NOW AMY

Elisabeth Ludbrook

BALBOA
PRESS

A DIVISION OF HAY HOUSE

Balboa Press books may be ordered through booksellers or by contacting:

Balboa Press
A Division of Hay House
1663 Liberty Drive
Bloomington, IN 47403
www.balboapress.com.au
1 (877) 407-4847

Print information available on the last page.

ISBN: 978-1-5043-0933-2 (sc)
ISBN: 978-1-5043-0938-7 (e)

Balboa Press rev. date: 09/08/2017

CHAPTER 1

THE SHED WAS half full of hay for the house cow. Amy snuggled herself into it and threw the brush onto the back shelf. She lay there watching Friska finish the last of his feed, gazing past him at the trees that grew along the fence line. There was almost no breeze, just enough to tickle the topmost leaves, they seemed to sparkle with their own light in the late afternoon sun.

She stretched out her arms, arching her young body into the hay. It smelled delicious. Bits of the stiff dry grass prickled her back. The pony's munching ceased for a brief moment as a long snort of contentment tumbled down his nostrils, scattering the light chaff up from the feed box and into his eyes, he blinked, shook his head and snorted again.

Friska was a light bay pony, with a black mane and tail. His fine legs were all black with not a white spot on him,

"You're looking good boy. We seem to have come through the summer unscathed. ."Amy said to herself, as she glanced into his feed box to see if he had finished his daily allotment of chaff and oats. "Not a mark on you. I must say, I got a bit worried when we hit that last spa at the Pakuranga Gymkhana last Saturday. Could have been nasty. But look at you." she hugged him around his neck. The pony let another snort escape from inside the now empty box. She ran her hand along his side and he swished his tail in response, if he could have purred he would have.

"Okay," Amy whispered to him. She threw his cover over his back, fastened it into place, opened the gate and hustled him into the wide paddock. After hanging the bridle over its hook, she set out for the house.

The dusty track wound through the ink weed and into the home orchard. Pears, apples and plum trees were beginning to be laden with fruit. Amy looked under the pear tree, searching for any fallen samples. The plums were almost over and soon her mother would be gathering the ripened apples and pears, turning them into preserves for the winter. It was a time of year that they all loved and they all turned out to help her. Father, mother and Amy would fill the large washing basket over and over again with the juicy fruit, and carry it into the large kitchen. For days her mother would wash and slice the fruit, while the big preserving pan stood on the stove, giving off its unmistakable sweet odours and the large glass jars, waiting to receive their contents, lay sterilising in the warm oven.

'Makes me feel like a squirrel' her mother would say.

Amy swung her way up the pathway to her home. She loved coming home. The house seemed to sit back smiling in the sun. It was a two-story timber house, with a wide verandah on two sides. She reckoned her Dad was very smart to have built their home with the verandahs to the side and back, where they caught the sun throughout the day. Most of the houses nearby had been built with handsome verandahs that faced the street.

'What's the use of that,' her Dad would say. 'Who wants to sit and look at the street when they can sit in the sun with wide green paddocks and these beautiful trees.'

The homestead kitchen opened onto the sunny, rear verandah. Amy ran up the steps and in through the open door. The kitchen was large. The walls, panelled with a dark timber, never failed to give her a sense of warmth and safety. A long table dominated the centre of the room and led to a wooden bench with a white enamel sink set in the centre. The wall above the sink held a clever timber rack, its many upright struts forming a firm, useful, draining frame. Plates of many different sizes sat waiting for their next use.

"Lo Mum!" She called as she entered the kitchen.

"Is that you m'darlin'?" came the familiar, out of site voice. "You get yourself out of those horse smelly clothes and into the bath. Dinner's just half an hour away."

Amy sniffed the warm cooking smells. The wood fired stove sat tucked into what had been a large fireplace. Her mother was very proud of the stove. Not for her she would say cooking as so many others still did, with iron pots hanging from iron bars cemented into their large fireplaces. The stove not only warmed the room but a system of pipes set into it heated the household hot water. Amy ran off to use just that in a warm bath.

*   *   *

The early sunshine lit up Amy's bedroom. It was too soon to warm it and an early autumn chill hugged the air.

'Seven-thirty already and Mum has not called me ... or maybe she called and I went back to sleep... cripes... I'll be late!'

Amy jumped from her bed, climbed quickly into her skirt and blouse and ran down the stairs. The table in the kitchen was laden with a selection of fruits, hot scones fresh from the oven, and large saucepan of porridge, from which her father was filling his bowl.

"Morning sweetheart. Jim from next door has brought in fresh cream, his Mum had more than she needed." He passed the cream jug to Amy. The large kitchen was already warm from the wood range, and the smell of baking filled all the corners of the room.

"There y'are m'darlin'." Amy's mother spoke in her soft Yorkshire accent, placing the steaming porridge before Amy and smiling her soft secret smile. "Y've plenty of time before school."

Her mother stood only five feet tall and at fourteen Amy was already a little taller. She loved the smell of her mother. Such a combination of soap and herbs and, well, just a mother smell. Amy looked at her mother. Katie's wide, short frame, was covered in her usual longer skirt and loose blouse with both garments hiding behind a large blue apron. As it so often did, her smile lifted the corners of her wide, generous mouth, and crept up her lovely face to settle behind her blue eyes. Often Amy was puzzled by that smile. It sat gently, almost permanently, on Katie's round face and the secret that seemed to lie behind it remained just that – a secret.

"And what is on for you today in school Amy?" her father asked. He smiled at her over his porridge enquiringly. "Is today a sport day?"

"Yes Daddy, we get to play basketball and then football. The boys play basketball with us and then we get to play rugby with them."

"Rugby, you still play that game with them? You must be getting too big by now for such sport. And there must be about what, eighty children in the school by now. How many seniors are there?"

Doug Brookfield looked at his daughter. Fourteen years old already, he thought. How did it happen so quickly? Why his Katie was not much older when he first met her. Only fifteen Katie had been. No it did not bear thinking about. Amy seemed to him too small for such rough sport. Her slender body and brown skinny arms....well they were not so skinny any longer but had plumped up considerably.

"You know how it works Daddy," Amy grinned through her porridge. "If we don't share each others sport then we don't get to play the games. There just are not enough of us for a decent game. There are only ten seniors and we are still not allowed to tackle when we play rugby. Mr. Bright refuses to let us, so we play a sort of tag game."

"Mr. Bright." chipped in Katie as she sat down to join them. "Ho, what a name for a Headmaster. Now tell me m'darlin', which is your favourite sport? That is when you can leave that pony of yours alone."

"Oh Mummy, I really do like rugby the best. You can run so much further and faster. It is just so tame on the basketball court being stuck to running inside those small areas. We haven't played much through the summer and I really get bored with playing cricket. If my friends didn't play and had not talked me into it I just would not bother. Actually," she grinned at them thinking about it "I much prefer baseball."

"Baseball?" Doug coughed. "what sort of baseball."

"They used to call it rounders. What a dumb name. Anyway baseball is so much fun. It's faster and everyone has to have a turn. You belt the ball and try and make a home run. Everyone runs to try and stop you."

"I think that I would like to see that." muttered her father. "I suppose that the boys play that as well?"

"Of course. They have too. None of us would have a team otherwise. And besides, they can hit it way farther than any of the girls. It would be nothing like as fast if it was just the girls but it is a summer game only and we are turning onto the winter games now."

Doug sipped his second cup of tea. Amy had left for school and he loved to have these minutes with Katie when his work would let him.

"Do you think that she is sport mad?"

Katie chuckled. "Well she doesn't get it from me."

"Maybe it is the New Zealand way. Maybe the whole country is sports mad it certainly seems so. I never heard of girls playing baseball. Do y'think that we just didn't have enough room back in the old country for so much sport. How do they get educated? You'd have to wonder."

"So she is strong and healthy and has a life we never had or imagined" Katie joined him with her tea. "She certainly spends time with that pony they are almost inseparable. She is up those hills on Dalebrooks farm all of her after school time. They are very good to her and let her have pretty much the run of the place."

"You don't think that she is, well, missing out on anything. Our family? Your parents my parents? Your sister Ellie and her children. You know how many cousins we had. Always somewhere to go. Always comfortable with each other and no shortage of good company to do things with."

"Don't do that Doug." Katie's voice dropped. "Yes we had a good life back home. And yes, York was a great town to live and grow up in but the war changed all that. Yes I miss 'em. But Doug I am very happy here in New Zealand. There are so many of us here. Runaways from England. Is that what they call us?" she looked around the kitchen room." this life is so much better than anything we would or could have had back home."

"Yes. - Yes you're right. The great war changed everything. So many who never came home. So many who were ruined both in health and mind when they did come home. I try not to think about it. We all came here. All of us wanting to get as far away from Europe as possible."

"We have good friends here Doug. The Plummers and the Robinsons and so many like them. Like us. Half of Ellerslie village are like us. Out here following the war, there is no going back."

The memories were stirring in Doug. Visions of people and noise and clutter came crowing in. Katie saw and got up and busied herself tidying up the breakfast dishes.

Doug looked down at his hands resting on the bright table cloth. They were thick strong hands cracked and rough from heavy outdoor work. He remembered how he had enlisted in the army in 1918. He had just turned eighteen and had gone straight down the road to the recruitment office. They would not let him in before he turned eighteen. He tried several times lying about his age but his father had known the recruitment officer and they kept him out. When he did finally join up the war was almost over. Not that anyone knew that at the time. Doug went to France for training and within four weeks it was all over.

And two years later when he turned twenty, he married Katie. They got married and came to New Zealand.

CHAPTER 2

THE ELLERSLIE VILLAGE sat close to the railway that linked the city of Auckland with the rest of the country. It was a small village surrounded by farmland and featured an assortment of wooden buildings that made up several shops, a Post Office and a large, double storied Hotel.

The school lay some distance from the main village area and with school over for the day, Amy and her best friend Pammy were heading there

"It all looks so quiet today." Pammy murmured as they wandered towards the small collection of shops. "I have thre'pence, shall we get a couple of ice-creams?"

"Hey yes!" Amy laughed. "Penny ones! And it's your turn!"

"Well you know I don't get much. Oh you are so lucky not to have brothers and sisters."

"Nah. Pammy. Y'know that your bunch are okay. It is just that you have too many of them!"

"Well I 'spose that I wouldn't change them. But seriously, they really drive me crazy sometimes. Charlie bosses me around all of the time and Maggie is forever looking in magazines at all of the glossy ladies."

"Do you look too?"

Pammy grinned. "Well er, yes I do. Actually they are fascinating. There's this film star in Europe called Marlene Dietrich. My Mum and Dad saw a film in the Ellerslie Picture House with Marlene Dietrich in it. Something called Angel in Blue or, oh yeah, Blue Angel. They wouldn't let us go with them. Too old for you they reckoned so we had to stay home with Maggie which is a bit of a nightmare as both James and Victor really play up. I just go to my room to get away from them." Pammy pause and looked at Amy as if to question her reaction. "And now" she went on,

"This lady has her photograph is in the magazines wearing trousers! What d'you think about that! Women in trousers!"

"Really? Oh how absolutely marvellous....! Trousers! What a truly sensible idea. I have to change all of the time into long pants when I want to ride Friska, and so many women still wear split skirts for riding. But trousers. Brilliant!"

"Well my Mum doesn't think so. You should hear her. Shameful state of women since the Great War, that's what she reckons. She says that women should be women and not try and copy men."

"Well, much as I like your Mum, I don't think that's right. I mean, look at it another way, how much more easily can you run, or ride, or row a boat when you are not slowed down with a skirt. Who invented skirts anyway? Where did that idea come from? It's like riding a horse side-saddle. What a super dumb idea that is. And whose idea was it? I'll bet women rode their horses astride until some stupid idiot decided that it was not proper and put us all into skirts, and, of all the most stupid things to do, put us side-saddle onto horses. Well I reckon that this French lady has got heaps of brains to put women in magazines into trousers."

"Goodness Amy. I never looked at it like that." Pammy giggled. "And she's not French she is German. Maybe they put women into skirts because it was easier for them to pee."

Both girls burst out laughing.

"Now that is not silly at all," said Amy through her chuckles. "It's probably right! I've never seen a man's things, but they must work very differently to ours 'cause all their pants open in front."

"You've never seen a man's things? Really?"

"Er... Well, It's all right for you Pammy, you have three brothers, but well," Amy blushed. "How am I supposed to know what a man looks like?"

"Well they're just TOTALLY different. That's all. C'mon, let's forget the whole thing. Anyway, here's the shop."

Together, the two girls entered the small, dark shop. A long counter ran the entire length of the room. All of the many articles needed for life on the farm were either sitting on shelves behind the counter, or hanging from hooks and rafters from the ceiling. Kerosene lanterns, spades, oilskins, all mixed in together amid cheese and potatoes, supplying the settlers' needs. Pammy spoke to the white-haired lady behind the counter. "Can we have two penny ice-creams, please."

Pammy had thick curly brown hair that seemed to grow in a springy wave from her head. Her lovely pale face was framed by its soft, bouncing mass. Pammy's hair, thought Amy, never seemed to fall out of place, not like her lighter, more golden, locks, that constantly fell in her eyes and seemed to stay permanently untidy. No matter how Amy tied the ribbons her mother ironed and laid out for her each morning, they would shake loose and drop her hair everywhere, usually long before lunchtime. She looked at her friend's gorgeous hair and sighed. Pammy was really lovely, with smooth white skin, and some very new bumps and hollows that had recently formed on her body, making her curvy and if Amy needed to find a word to describe her, it would have to be 'delicious'.

Together they wandered on, peering in the shop windows at the display of goods.

"Ouch!" gasped Amy. A small stone hit her right in the centre of her back. "Ouch again," she said rubbing the spot.

"Ooh," echoed Pammy." What's that!" She ducked quickly as a small missile flew over her head. The two girls looked behind them. There were only a few people in the street, a mother and small child coming out of the grocers, and an older man creeping home with his newspaper.

"What was that?" Amy looked at Pammy. "Who threw that?" She turned again to look. Not a soul was to be seen. "I could swear that someone biffed those small stones at us. What do you think?"

Pammy shrugged. "We could creep around behind the dairy, and down that alley. We could soon see from there if anyone has been taking pot shots at us." The two girls ducked into the alley. It ran in a narrow, dusty pathway between the boarded buildings.

"Quick! Under here," Amy grabbed her friends hand and pulled her down and under a large wooden platform with several bins placed on its top. A small, protective roof poked out above a door that opened onto the platform, shutting out the sunlight and adding a dreary look to its unpainted appearance. They waited, Amy listened closely, cautioning Pammy to keep quiet with a finger to her lips.

Peeping round the side of the bin, Pammy nudged Amy, and pointed at the corner of the building. Creeping as quietly as possible, glancing both right and left, a tall boy came into sight.

"Good Grief!" Amy and Pammy looked at each other in superised disbelief.

"He is about the last person I would ever have expected to pull a mean stunt." Pammy whispered.

"WELL!" cried Amy, jumping to her feet with her hands going onto her hips. "So! Tom Sigley! WHAT do you think you are doing?"

Pammy jumped up with her, "I bet you threw those stones at us! You mean pooh! I'm gonna tell your sister Janet!"

Tom looked up with a sudden start. Guilt sat all over his face and body. His gangly long arms jerked with surprise as he spun round to face them. He pushed away his guilt and then, feigning bravado, burst out laughing.

"Tell Janet? H...H...Ho. That's a good one Pammy! Tell Janet! What would she do? What would you tell her anyway? You think that she would dob me in? Rubbish... and besides," he added, "I have so much untold 'don't-mention-it' stuff on her, she wouldn't dare dob me in."

Amy said nothing. Tom Sigley was pretty harmless really. It was a bit of a mystery why he had thrown stones at them but he had definitely been acting strangely lately. Like herself, Tom was fourteen years old. He had grown fast and his long body seemed to be able to bend in all directions. His clear, honest, blue eyes sparkled with life, and dark hair grew thickly from his smooth forehead requiring his mother to sit him frequently at the kitchen table, where, with a mock French accent, and a long, low bow, she would wave him to the chair declaring

"Ahh, Monsure, parley vous der queek trim?"

Tom's smile was infectious, showing strong, straight white teeth that beamed out from his face. Many times his smile had turned a difficult situation into one that was easily forgotten, and at this moment, for Tom, that same smile was not working at all on the two girls facing him.

Amy studied him closely. Throwing stones? Now if it had been that new boy, Ben Hartley, that would be more likely, he was a pretty mean kid, but Tommy? Nah!

"Tommy?" she asked, taking her hands from her hips and folding her arms, "Why did you toss those stones at us?"

"Yah!" Tom started to taunt, then, faced suddenly with a soft, questioning version of Amy, instead of an angry one, he turned a bright red.

"Come on Tommy," she coaxed," It's not like you. You're not mean."

Tom tried to turn on his reliable grin, but instead his face seemed to turn even more red. He looked down at the ground, digging at it with his bare foot. Suddenly he turned and ran out of the alley disappearing onto the main road, and was gone.

"Now that's weird!" said Pammy. "That's really weird. What's biting that boy, Tommy Sigley? You usually can't get a word out of him. Those small stones can really hurt!"

Amy was very quiet. H'mm she thought. Tommy Sigley was certainly different lately. He would sit just behind her in the school assembly. Or he would bump into her when they were playing games. She suddenly felt a surge of warmth for him. The whole episode seemed slightly pathetic.

"Let's forget it Pammy. There's no harm done. It's probably just a stupid prank he felt like doing and it's not as if there was a whole gang of them. I know that that new boy Ben Hartley and some of the others ganged up on the smaller kids when they were walking home last week. They took little Maurice Manley's school bag and ran off with it. They dumped it in a drain full of water and the little boy got wet through getting it back. The little kid cried all the way home. It must have taken his Mum days to dry it out."

"I didn't know that!" said Pammy. "What a nasty thing to do. How could they! They are so much bigger than the little kids. I'll never be the same towards that boy Ben again. AND I had been feeling sorry for him 'cause being new must have felt strange to him!" She frowned at the trees as they walked on through the village.

CHAPTER 3

Tom Sigley ran heading for his home. It was a good mile to run. The road was dust and metal leading from the village. It ran directly west towards a distant hill. The hill stood alone, covered in open green pasture with just one lone tree sitting, rather sadly, on the summit. He loved to run this stretch of road and his bare feet, toughened by years of this same activity, seemed to hardly feel the sharp stones on the surface.

He was furious with himself. Damn Damn Damn! That was a good shot he had made hitting Amy in the centre of her back. Too bad that Pammy had ducked just when the second stone would have hit her. Dammit! Why hadn't Amy stayed angry at him! How unfair of her not to stay angry. Then he could've dumped dirt on their school bags or done something, he really was not sure what, to taunt them. Get a reaction.....you can't dump anything on someone who doesn't get angry with you. Pammy got angry! Dammit Amy, you're not fair. Tom swung his bag at the tall grass beside the road. He had wanted to make her angry. More than anything he had wanted to make her angry though he did not know why. Just get a reaction. He slowed down suddenly no longer in a hurry to reach his destination. His breathing had hardly altered from running and his long legs changed to a happy lope eating up the remainder of the distance. There would be the cow to milk when he got home.

His older brother William met him at the gate. Tall with wide shoulders, brown hair, and a face not unlike Tom's, he swung the gate open to let Tom through.

"You're late." he accused. "It's your turn to milk old Mugs, and Dad's in an almighty tiz."

"Yah right!" muttered Tom pushing past.

You never knew with William. He would say things like that, and more often than not, it would be untrue. It made Tom distrust him. William was sixteen, and if he could shirk any of the many chores that needed to be done on the small farm, he would do so. William was a bit of a bully, but Tom could always dodge away and easily out run him. Usually he was too lazy to chase you for long. It was different now. Tom was getting bigger. His Mother kept tut-tutting that he was growing out of his clothes faster than she could hand them down from William, that, together with how much he ate were, it seemed, her favourite subjects.

'Y'cant fill 'im.' she kept saying.

It would not take long to milk old Mugs, he thought, she had much less milk at night.

The Sigley home was a small, three bedroom cottage set back near the creek. In the early years his Mum had done all of her washing in that creek but now she had a copper and a proper wash house that his father had built and it made her work much easier. His Dad kept a large vegetable garden inside a fenced area near the creek. He was constantly pottering around down there, where everything they needed was grown in the rich volcanic soil. The mild climate allowed the prolific garden to keep them supplied with food all the year round.

"Well lad." Tom's father stood on the top step looking down at him. "Get yourself changed and fed, a man's got to get all the work done between sun up and sun down."

Tom grinned at his father. He really loved the old man. Well he had always seemed old! His Dad had been in the Great War and he limped from a bullet wound in his left leg; a legacy of his time in the trenches of France. Better that than some others, he would say, but it made Tom, seeing the difficulty and pain that the old man tried to hide, want to help him as much as he could.

CHAPTER 4

AMY AND PAMMY wandered through the Ellerslie village. Tom's strange behaviour still sat with Amy. She could not feel rankled by it but actually felt almost happy that he had gone to so much trouble. He had definitely been waiting for them while he hid behind the dairy. She wanted to laugh but glancing at Pammy decided to keep it to herself. Pammy was still fuming over Ben Hartley's bullying of the smaller boys. Amy bumped into her when she stopped suddenly before a shop window.

"Gosh Amy, look at this the Ellerslie races are coming. Now THAT would be gorgeous time to see ladies in all the fancy clothes that Maggie drools over."

"Don't say fancy. Say elegant. Or beautiful. I mean --- ? Fancy? What sort of word is …Oh!" Amy stopped and gasped. "Oh Pammy look!" The two girls stood before a large shop window. In the centre of the window, a large green poster dominated its surroundings, beaming out onto the street at eye level, for all to see.

ELLERSLIE RACE DAY

SATURDAY 11th MAY 1935

FIRST RACE STARTS AT 10.00 AM
ENTRY 2/6d. PER PERSON

10.00 A.M.	Amateur Gentleman rider over four furlongs.
10.30 A.M.	Two mile handicap
11.00 A.M.	Ladies One Mile Steeplechase.
11.30 A.M.	Maiden Thoroughbred One Mile Race

LUNCH

1.00 P.M.	One and one half Mile Steeplechase. Open to all.
1.30 P.M.	Champion Two Year Old half Mile.
2.00 P.M.	Open Champion over two Miles.
2.30 P.M.	Last Race: Consolation Entries Five Furlongs

Tea and Biscuits available at the Tea Tent.

A Ladies Mile Race at Ellerslie! And a steeplechase at that! A surge of excitement ran through Amy as she read the words through for a second time. Ellerslie races. The local race meetings took place some three times a year. An autumn meeting then one in the spring and an extra large one in the summer at the New Year. It was a favourite break for the work weary settlers. Amy had several times in the past attended with her parents these popular local social outings. Children parents grandparents, everyone loved the races. And the sign sat there in front of her. Beckoning and taunting. Like some hypnotic magnet it sat in the centre of the shop window.

The Ellerslie races. Oh how Friska would love that. She could enter him in the event. Her mind raced at the thought. He could win it. I know he could win it. He loves to run fast. If I remember the Ladies Mile race from last year the course goes over a big hill, and Friska goes faster than ever up the hills. He just loves the hills.

"Amy!" cried Pammy with dispare. "You're thinking you want to ride Friska in this race?"

"Yes," whispered Amy. That's the trouble with best friends, she thought, they know you so well!

"But Amy, how can you and Friska go in such a race, you're only fourteen. They'd never let you!"

Amy stared at the pavement and muttered defensively.

"Lots of Jockeys are only fourteen."

"Yes, but they're boys. Stablehands are boys. My uncle Ben runs a stable over in Avondale he has lots of stablehands. And anyway your father would never let you. You're too small. Probably Friska is too small as well."

Pammy raced on, more afraid of her friend's adventurous streak than she knew, wanting to turn Amy's mind from such a fool hardy thing before the idea took hold.

Amy's thoughts ran from the pavement she stood on to her pony and to the sensation of flying over the streams and fallen tree trunks on their hill top rides together. In a flash like a lightning bolt the image of winning the race hit her mind momentarily catching her off guard. She had to bite her tongue to stop blurting out her thoughts to Pammy. She needed to think about this, however, think or not, her mind was already made up.

"Perhaps you're right," she mumbled to Pammy, keeping her fingers crossed inside her pockets. "Anyway, I have to go. Thanks for the ice-cream."

* * *

Amy walked on home deep in thought. It was five weeks before the race meeting and they had plenty of time to prepare. The last few years of constantly riding and competing in the local shows had really become pretty boring. You could not race around much at the Shows. There was always some steward or official waving their sticky finger and demanding that you slow down. Would it cost much to enter the race? Would her Daddy let her ride? He has to, she told herself. Friska can win. I know he can.

That evening as they sat around the dining table, Amy crossed her fingers for good luck and tried to keep her voice casual in a make-conversation kind of way.

"Daddy, I see that there's an Ellerslie Race Meeting coming in May."

"Aye mi darlin', that there is. We will all be going, you know how we love the local races, let us hope for a fine day this year shall we."

Doug Brookfield stood at just six feet in his socks, with broad shoulders and strong arms. He always felt as if had been made especially large and strong to look after his two girls, that is, until he made the occasional visit to the local pub, which soon changed his thinking. His mates soon pulled him down to normal size. When the Maori shearers were in town you could add another three inches to the height of the men he knew. He smiled to himself and brought his attention back to Amy. She sat with excitement written all over her face.

"Daddy, can I ride Friska in the Ladies Mile race?" Amy blurted out. "Oh Daddy, he just loves to run. We can win the Ladies Mile race I know we can. I have been thinking about it all day... well ever since I saw the notice that is... Friska is so fast up hill and he is very fit we could build up more speed and strength between now and the May races!"

A stunned silence met her outburst. Oh cripes, how could I be so stupid, she told herself sharply, she just had not been able to keep the words in. She sat on her crossed fingers. Oh no, she thought. Oh cripes, now you've done it. You and your big mouth. Please God, she blinked to keep the thoughts inside her. Please don't let him blow his top. She wished the floor boards would open up and swallow her.

Doug and Katie looked at each other across the table. Katie's head gave a tiny 'no' shake. So tiny that you could scarcely see the movement. They knew and understood each other, the private, unspoken language between them often filled and charged the whole room. It filled the room now.

"Amy, Amy." Her Father shook his head. "You have no idea what you're asking. No idea at all! Ride in the Ladies Mile Race! That IS a crazy idea. The other lady riders will be much older than you and their horses are big thoroughbreds. Friska would not stand a chance against them. Those big horses take great long strides when they run and the fences in that steeplechase are high. Friska's legs are way to much shorter and his strides only half the distance of those bigger horses. What on earth made you ask such a thing?"

"But Daddy," Amy pleaded. "Friska loves to run fast. You can feel it in him. And he just seems to speed up when we run the long hill. Why he ..."

"Enough! Big horses and big fences!" Doug was appalled. She was too young. She was too little. The horse was too little. "We will not speak of this again. I cannot think what has gotten into you to suggest such a thing...uh." he held up is hand stopping her as her next outburst tried to jump out. "NOT another word. Ridiculous... So off to bed with you young lady and no more nonsense." the thought of his only daughter racing over the demanding Ellerslie steeplechase track, filled Doug with fear. She was not ready. She was absolutely not ready.

Amy sat dejectedly on the edge of her bed, her fists pounding on her knees. What to do she thought. She climbed in under the blankets, but her mind would not stop. She could feel herself and Friska, galloping up the long hill that dominated the race course and swinging effortlessly over the fences. They really were not that high, she told herself, merely brush jumps that encouraged the horses to keep a fast pace over them. In her mind Friska appeared to speed up, determinately faster as the hill became tougher. How could she tell him that they were not allowed to race? She had had such a long talk with him about it that evening as she gave him his feed. So tuned in to each other they were that the pony seemed to register her thoughts and give his approval. Could he out run bigger horses? Of course he could. They had done it many times before fooling around at the horse Shows. They called him a pony, but really he was a borderline size at fourteen hands high he could class as a horse. There were plenty of small horses that could out run the bigger ones. Plenty of them did so she told herself....Amy sat bolt upright in the bed as a new thought hit her. Her father had not actually said that she could not enter and ride in the race. Oh, he had said lots of things, like it was a crazy idea, and that she did not know what she was asking, but at no time had he actually forbade her to enter and ride. Not once had he actually said ....NO you cannot ride ...She snuggled further under the blankets smiling to herself.

"Friska and I are going to win the Ladies Mile race at Ellerslie!" she whispered to herself before sleep finally took over.

CHAPTER 5

ON HER WAY home from school the following day, Amy made a detour to the nearby Ellerslie racecourse. A high stone wall separated the race course from the road, and she walked along beside it to a pair of imposing iron gates. The gates were lying open. She simply walked in. Beautifully well kept gardens of flowers and trees greeted her and the excitement inside began to tie knots in her stomach as she made her way along the white shell path towards the nearest building she could see, a large roofed in grandstand.

The race course was nestled amongst green hills with clumps of tall native forest in the surrounding gullies. Occupying over sixty acres, it ran over a flat open space rising to a long hill on the south eastern side. The track itself looked to be in three parts. An open wide strip of grass with a white timber rail built at waist height, encircled the track area. A branch of track veered off to the left to run in a further direction up a long hill, descending on the eastern side to rejoin the lower track. Across from where Amy stood, a short, two hundred yard stretch linked into the main track creating an extension to a side area where most of the races were started. It was the best racecourse in the country. Amy could not help but feel both nervous at what she was about to do and excited by her surroundings Houses had begun to be built beyond the racecourse boundary on the hillside above the long hill as the nearby Auckland city grew constantly outward. An attractive stone wall on the western side of the track had been built, and a new, smaller, grandstand added. Its modern architecture looked out of place beside the rather grand design of the original two-storey grandstand. Amy found a low gate in the railing and wandered in towards the building, not quite knowing what to do. She spotted three men, officials of the track, leaning together against a sunlit wall on the other side of a large lawn, and by what seemed to be a row of open, individual horse stalls.

"Hello there," the tall thin one called. "Are you looking for someone, Miss?"

"Yes, please." Amy tried hard to look taller and older but she was quite suddenly feeling even more nervous. "Is there and office or somewhere that you can get information about the May races?" She was suddenly very glad of the many times that she had needed to visit the Official tent that the horse shows and gymkanas always had set up close to the show ring. All of your event entries had to be made there and Amy hoped that the same was true for horse races.

The tall thin man left his companions and walked towards her. He had a deeply tanned face and long laugh lines ran from beside his nose to the corners of his mouth. He smiled kindly at her and Amy felt her stomach relax.

"Yes there is an office. Over there at the back of the main grandstand" he waved his hand in the direction of the large building. "It's not open just now. Closes each day at four o'clock. Unless it is race time that is. Open all day the week of the races."

"Oh." Amy's voice dropped. It was already past that time although the warm sun made it seem less so'

"Perhaps we can help you?" he continued kindly. "What is it you are looking for."

"Umm," she was beginning to feel lost and rather foolish. It was all so unknown. She wanted to turn and run back the way that she had come. Get a grip she told herself swallowing hard.

"Well I was hoping to enter my pony er horse in the Ladies Mile race on the ... in the May races... and I ...I just thought that if I came here I would find out how to ... or that is where I needed to go to enter him in the race." she looked at him hopefully. "Is there somewhere that I need to go?"

A second man moved over to join them. He was as short as his friend was long and it struck Amy that his body seemed thick and solid from his ears down to his surprisingly small feet. His neck did not exist but disappeared into his shoulders and his barrel like chest made his walk unwieldy but his short bowed legs gave him away. An ex-jockey, more at home on a horse than on his feet.

"Hello little lady." he smiled at her with a fun, Santa Claus smile. "Vic MacKays the name and who might you be." he held out a strong, stubby fingered hand.

Completely taken aback, Amy gulped. She had never shaken hands with anyone before. She held out her hand rather self conspicuously, completely unsure of what might happen next. Vic MacKay took her hand and the warmth of the man flowed through him making Amy feel suddenly very happy. Her shyness and apprehension completely fell away as she looked at the warm face. Brown sparkling eyes seemed to peep knowingly at her from half closed lids helping her feel comfortable and unafraid.

"Er... I'm Amy." she offered. She did not want to tell him her full name. Everyone knew each other here in Ellerslie and she desperately wanted no one to know what she was doing. "please," she asked him "can you tell me how much it would cost to enter my pony er…my horse in the Ladies Mile Race on the eleventh of May."

"Hmm. A pony is a bit small for such a long race." Vic said as his companions smiled nodding to each other knowingly.

"Oh but he is fourteen two hands, he is a horse really" Amy blurted. "And he is so very fast, even on the wet ground and he just gets faster up hills! He just loves to run, and please, I really have to enter him in the race."

"Well. You are an unexpected visitor with an unexpected request. How old are you? I haven't seen you here before. There are restrictions on entry into the May races although I must say, actually… " Vic glanced at the two other men. "The restrictions are pretty flexible," he continued after several long, silent seconds. "We have everything coming from flash, highly-trained thoroughbreds to Maori brumbies ridden bareback."

"I am fourteen." Amy answered indignantly her awkwardness

forgotten "and my pony, er horse, is not anything like a Maori brumby or any other brumby for that matter, he is a trained hunter and he is very fast."

The three men chuckled.

"Brumbies they may be," added the tall thin one rubbing his chin. "But run a good race they surely do. Some of those Maori boys from the coast are brilliant riders. Some of 'em are awful. Y'can tell straight away who is any good and who is not. So is it that you will be riding your...er...horse yourself?"

"B..but of course. I always ride him I couldn't have anyone else ride him.

Oh please she whispered silently to herself closing her eyes, please let them let me do this.

"Well why not." the tall thin man grinned. "There have been plenty of gutsy fourteen year old jockeys in the past. All boys mind you but why not a girl. Okay, little Miss it will cost ten shillings to enter your pony in the race and the entries close Thursday next week. You can purchase an entry ticket from the office here at the track. Do you live nearby? Some of our race entries come from as far away as Hamilton and the boys from the coast well they ride their horses in eighty miles the day before. How far do you come? Will your pony, I mean horse, need an overnight paddock? We put most of 'em up here on the track and some go down to Sigley's. Old man Sigley is a great horseman and looks after all the coast Maori boys."

"Oh no. Thank you." Amy hoped he would not ask too many questions. She hoped even more, that he would not recognise her as Douglas Brookfield's daughter. The last thing she needed was for any word to get out of what she was doing. Amy's throat and chest felt very tight as her nervousness returned. "M-my home is not far. And I can easily ride in on the morning of the race."

"Well then." The man named Vic grinned wider. "That's settled then".

"Thank you, Oh thank you." Amy gripped her hands to keep herself from hugging him. "I will be back here with the money before next Thursday."

Amy walked the pathway back to Ellerslie village. She plunged her hands deep into her pockets unaware of her surroundings, her feet automatically finding their way. Deep in thought she gazed at the ground. Now where do I get ten shillings from? She mused. I cannot go to either Mum or Dad. Maybe I could draw it from my savings account. The sixpence Mum gives me each week for the savings account should have built up by now. Can I draw it out without her finding out? You never know with Mum. She somehow always knows things, even when you haven't told her anything. I don't know how she does it but she just 'knows'. What to do, what to do …? Amy spotted a log just off the path, basking in a shaft of sunlight that poured through the trees singling it out from the shaded surroundings. She homed in on the log, sat in the sunlight and pulled her Post Office Savings book from her school bag. All of the children carried them. The savings were made once a week through the school as a part of the programme to encourage the children to learn about saving. Amy opened the small, official looking book … 8/6d. Only eight shillings and sixpence! Not enough, nowhere near enough … what can I do? There has to be a way because I know that we will ride in this race. It just IS..... Maybe I can sell something? I dunno, flowers? Mum would know straight away. Horse dung for gardens? Hardly. Everyone has a horse or nearly everyone. Janice Cotterill's family don't have a horse and neither do the Whinchcombe's. But then, there are so many horses around. They still tie them up to the rails in the street, and the horses dump their big poos right there, so anyone can pick it up for free if they want it on their gardens. Her mind rambled on in search of a way but to no avail. 'Thanks buddy,' she muttered as she patted the log. Amy swung her feet back onto the path and kicked at stones, watching them fly in all directions, as she headed for home.

"Y'know God", she whispered to the air. "You and I both know that we will be in the Ladies Mile Race in May. Only five weeks away. I need to know how to get the entry fee money it's only ten shillings but seems like a lot of money. How can I get some? You only get four shillings in prize money when you win the riding events in the local Show it doesn't go far. So I'm calling on you to let me know how to get the money. I am going to need it pretty soon so as not to miss out on the entry so let me know soon," she urged.

Feeling better, she began to run. It was great to run after being lumbered with such heavy thinking. Suddenly the excitement of being able to ride in the race took hold of her. She ran faster feeling lighter than the air itself. Amy forced herself to slow down going through the village where the local people could become alarmed and call her to slow down, as adults do, if she kept her pace at break-neck speed. Once through the village, and onto the short road home, she sped up again, delighting again in the feeling of her own speed. Now it was up to God she reckoned to send her the direction she needed to take. It felt good to run, released from making a decision of what to do for the moment, she ran on, her school bag bouncing and the wind whistling past her ears.

That night, Amy climbed into bed. Sleep seemed impossible. She had not received any answers, or inspiration from God. Just nothing. She rolled out of her bed and pushed the windows open. They were fold-back windows that slid back on small rails, leaving a wonderful wide open space and often Amy would leave her bed and lean on the window sill, content to simply gaze out over the tops of the trees, silhouetted by the moon.

It was just a blank. Nothing. No ideas, nothing. She looked into the night sky the trees were all soft and moody in the moonlight. With a deep sigh, she turned back to bed.

It made little difference. Still no answers. She wriggled around under the blankets turning to gaze towards her dressing table. A silver thimble, a gift from her grandmother in England for her fourteenth birthday, caught her eye. It shone in the moonlight beside her hairbrush. It was supposed to be a special thing to have a silver thimble. Something women gave women, she had forgotten the reason why … Could she sell it? A silver thimble was quite expensive, and in New Zealand in 1935 there were less of these English pieces, or so she had been told. Could she sell it? Was it worth anything? Jumping from the bed Amy picked up the thimble. It looked as if it had never been used. How could anyone want to sit and sew when there was so much to see and do? It looked brand new. She pulled open the top drawer. A blue silk scarf lay folded on top of its contents. She lifted it out. It is really very lovely, she thought, a gift from her aunt Lydia in London. Lydia from London. Huh. She thought, now that has a ring to it. She put the thimble and the scarf into a paper bag and looked around the room. A small, exquisite china flower vase sat on top of the corner bookshelves. Amy stuffed it into the paper bag before she lost her courage and thought too hard about what she was doing. She put the bag back on the dressing table and climbed back into bed. My Mum will kill me, she thought as sleep then came easily …

CHAPTER 6

THE SCHOOL DAY seemed to drag by. Everything today was in slow motion. She had run out of the house that morning and her mother had to call her back.

"Amy! Come back." Katie had called."Y've forgotten your lunch"

The brown paper bag was tucked inside her school bag with the three pieces that hopefully, who knows would turn into ten shillings for the entry money. How could she get rid of Pammy and go into the village on her own? The after-school rush of children going home left no room for slipping away alone.

"Amy Brookfield!" Amy jumped in her seat as the Headmaster sharply called her name.

"Er.. Yes Sir?" Her voice came out croaky and crooked.

"What was the date we have just been discussing? When did Horatio Nelson actually invade France, and if so what was the Battle of Waterloo?"

He has seen through me totally, Amy thought, I was miles away. She was sitting beside Pammy at her school desk and her thoughts had been totally with the immediate question of how to get away without any holdups.

"Er – Horatio who Sir?"

"Come on Amy. Be good enough to give me your attention. You

have the answer written in your last night's homework. Now, can I have an answer?"

Half a dozen hands went into the air.

"I'm glad to see that SOME of my time has not been completely wasted. Yes Janice? Can you give me the answer?"

"I can't come with you tonight, Amy." Pammy packed her school bag. "It's my music lesson night and I have to be at Mrs. Goodhue's by ten to four."

Amy felt relief flood through her. It had bothered her all day. How was she to get into Ellerslie without Pammy. She could never try and sell the things with Pammy there, her friend would instantly see what she was up to.

"Okay Pammy, we can go in together tomorrow night I had forgotten that it was your music night."

"So long," called Pammy as she stuffed her books into her bag and hurried out the door. "See you tomorrow."

Amy packed her school bag slowly. The hustle and activity around her seemed endless as everyone tried to grab their bags at the same time, eager to put the school day behind them. She hung back as others ran out of the school gate.

"Hey Amy." her friend Elaine called to her. "You want to come to my place and see the puppies our dog had last night?"

Amy liked Elaine. She was bold and fun and Amy often visited her nearby home.

"Your dog Eight has had puppies? Really?"

"She had eight puppies last night. That's how she got her name anyway. She was one of a litter of eight. Maybe you could have one."

"Oh Elaine you know how much I would love to have one." Amy was tempted to go with her friend; very tempted. She dug her fingernails into the palms of her hands to get herself back from the new wanting. She had to take her opportunity today it could not be left until tomorrow. No.

"Can I come with you tomorrow? There's something I really need to do and I can't put it off. Would it be okay if I came with you after school tomorrow? I would love to see the puppies. Eight puppies. Cripes… is that a lot?"

"Yes it is a lot, but sometimes dogs have even more than that in a litter. It's okay Amy, let's see them tomorrow." Elaine walked with her out of the school gate, and waved a good bye as she turned and headed off towards her home.

Amy was decidedly nervous. Would anyone buy her pieces? What a distraction it had been talking to Elaine. She pulled her thoughts back from the picture of eight small puppies to the paper bag in her school bag. Don't think about it, she told herself. Just do it!

Amy entered the Ladies' dress shop on Ellerslie's Main road. "Excuse me please."

A large, grandmotherly figure turned and peered over the counter at her.

"Well. What can we do for you young lady?" She sounded bored as if sensing that Amy was not likely to be a paying customer and that the sooner that she went away the better.

"I would like to sell these pieces." Amy reached into her paper bag and lifted the three pieces onto the counter. She felt ridiculous. She felt small and childish as the pieces took on a new look, quite different from the promise they had made in her room last night. Back then it had all made perfect sense.

"My Aunt sent this silk scarf all the way from London …"

"Sorry my sweet." The large-faced grandmother interrupted. "We don't buy outside the chosen producers. Have to watch the sharks you know. The vase is very pretty but we really have no place for it here."

"Oh." Amy felt as if she had shrunk even smaller. "Thank you," she mumbled as she turned and stumbled out of the shop. The large-faced grandmother watched her go.

Amy drew her breath. She dug her fingernails into the palms of her hands and walked on looking into the other shops. There were five shops in the Ellerslie village apart from the familiar grocers. Amy tried the next shop where a mixed assortment of household goods were displayed in the window. Vases, chairs, mirrors, tables. The faded, gold lettering on the window read *ELLERSLIE ANTIQUES.*

A man and a woman stood chatting behind the counter. The shop was full of items, bits and pieces of the many items crowded in on each other as if struggling to breathe. The whole place smelled dusty. The woman behind the surprisingly uncluttered counter was young and smartly dressed, the middle aged man with her looked, in an ill fitting grey suit, decidedly shabby.

"Good afternoon, Miss." he said in tones designed to impress his companion. "How can we help you today?"

"Please Sir." Amy gathered up her courage. "I would like to sell these pieces." She took the articles from the paper bag and placed them on the glass counter.

The man and woman looked on as the items were placed, one by one, on the counter. The scarf, the thimble and lastly, the vase. They glanced at each other and then looked back at the pieces.

Amy looked too. They looked so small and lonely. Nothing like they had looked at home.

The shabby man glanced again at his companion.

"My dear," he said with condescending tones," we cannot take on any more stock. We really are overloaded at present and this slump has left people with very little spending money. Perhaps later on into the summer when Christmas is close. But just now? Well. Sorry."

Amy bundled the three pieces into the paper bag. She felt sillier than ever. She walked into the street forgetting to thank them. It was a relief to get back onto the pavement and into the sunshine.

Drat and drat and drat! Now what? Looking up and down the street she told herself. Come on, it surely cannot get much worse!

It was a men's shop. It sold felt hats and jackets, pipes and shooting sticks. It was the least likely shop of all to buy her pieces. Well... what is there to lose now, she asked herself and went in.

The man behind the counter was surprised to see a young girl enter his shop. The counter was small, leaving more room for the clothing racks that turned the rather cramped shop into what seemed to be a forest of men's clothing.

"Well. Aren't you a delightful surprise to brighten up a bored man's day. And what pray brings you to my clothing shop? Father's birthday coming up? For sure it is too soon for Christmas," he chuckled in a way that made Amy love him on the spot. All her previous inhibitions vanished as his smile went straight to her heart.

"Er... Well Sir, I um-- I want to sell my pieces. They are very good pieces and almost hardly used."

"Pieces are they?" he chuckled again, as if she was both acceptable and fun. The feeling relaxed her and she loved him even more. "Well come on. Let's have a look."

Amy placed the three pieces onto the counter adding a quick aside to God as she did so. Help me here she silently asked him, I am needing a bit of help. For some minutes the shop man looked at them without speaking, and the objects started to look even more small and silly. Amy watched him gaze down on them. She started to speak, to tell him they really were valuable, but all of a sudden she dared not to speak at all and just stood there in silence. She felt nothing. Nothing at all.

"So tell me little sweetheart." He looked across at her, his eyes twinkled and she felt still more comfortable with him. "What is it you will be needing the money for?"

"Oh, um," Amy was unprepared for such a direct question. Before she could think she found herself telling him all about the Ladies Mile Race, he looked so interested that she just couldn't stop herself. She told him all about Friska, and seeing the Race Meeting notice in the window. She even told him of her father and mother and as her tongue ran on she found herself saying how she just knew, knew, knew... that this was so right for her.

Her new friend listened intently. He looked again at her for a long time, then straightened up. "Hmm. Indeed hmm. Well I am going to share a secret with you. Let me see now, how old are you? About fourteen?"

Amy nodded. She had no idea what was to come, but she felt comfortable and trusting with him.

"It is a while ago now, but when I was sixteen, I wanted more than anything to ride my horse in the local races. Didn't live in Ellerslie back then, we lived in Morrinsville and it was quite a racing centre. So I trained my horse up. Jumping out of his skin he was. A beaut half thoroughbred. You could breed 'em with the wild horses back then. The Hauraki plains were full of the wild horses, my mate and I used to go after them on occasions and round up dozens. Sell 'em off. But I liked to keep the odd good looker and train 'em up. We made some good money. Loved the life yes sireee."

"Oh. What a lovely thing to do. I would love a life like that."

"You're a spunky little thing, aren't you?" He chuckled again. "A bit of spunk can get us into all sorts of trouble in this life. All sorts of trouble. But then …," he paused as if remembering many things then snapped himself back to the present and to his young visitor. "But, what the hell. It would be a dull and boring life without it. Eh, young lady? What's your name by the way?"

"I'm Amy Brookfield." She answered dutifully. "I live with my Mum and Dad along past the main road corner."

"Well we all know the corner. Been calling it that for a long time now. So you must be Doug Brookfield's girl. You do a bit of Show Ring riding at the A and P each year. I take the family along we like to go. I watch the horses but the kids you just can't keep em away from the merry go round."

"Oh yes." She felt glad that he was no longer a stranger. "My Dad shows his Clydesdales each year. He does contract work with them."

"Ahh, yes … Beautiful horses are Clydesdales. Don't ya just love the bigness and the strength of them?"

"Oh I do." She warmed towards him even more. "Dad feeds and grooms them. Sometimes you would think that they were his extra children. He really fusses over them."

"Well he has to Amy. They are his bread and butter. We are just coming out of the biggest slump the world has seen in modern times, a man needs his income and those great horses are his income."

"What happened to keep you from riding your horse in the local races?" She did not feel at all embarrassed to ask him such a personal question on such a short acquaintance and he did not seem to mind. He was enjoying the exchange.

"Oh yeah… That. Well sweetheart. The Great War came. Yep nineteen-fourteen. All good and able-bodied men to fight for King and country… frivolities such as local race meetings were put on hold while the boys went off to fight. Yep, fight the good fight. That's what they said. And so it was. They cancelled the races and I joined up. Went off in a troop ship to sunny Greece."

"But you came back and the war has been over for years."

"I suppose it is years. Sometimes it seems like a chapter in a book you've read - like a sort of past life, you know that you were there but there are times when it seems all a dream. Not a pleasant experience. Oh no. Nasty business. Ya lose a lot of buddies, ahh whatta waste but this is where we are today. The sun is shining and we have plenty to eat so on the whole you can't complain."

"But you could sti …"

"Oh no me darlin'. Nah…" He stopped her where she was and pulled up his trouser leg and there were his leg should have been, was a leg made of wood. It looked hard and unwieldy, and his long black socks rose up from his shiny black shoes, as if hugging a stiff post, the wood made a hollow sound as he patted it. "I call 'im Benjamin Franklin and this little companion holds me upright."

Amy was stunned. She had never seen a wooden leg. She had heard about them but never, well… it looked so clumsy. She gasped, and he quickly covered it up again.

"Ach! I can still ride horses, but I can't race 'em."

"Oh. Oh how awful."

"Awful? Nah. Some of those boys, the ones who made it home, well… " His voice dropped a little as he remembered. "Well they are not all in great shape. A man's lucky to be hail and hearty, can enjoy a pint and love his Missus. Life goes on."

Amy could think of nothing to say. She could not imagine having only one leg. God gave you two legs. What sort of life could you expect

34

if you could not ride or run? They were both silent for several minutes, the atmosphere settled heavily between them, each alone with their own thoughts.

He broke the spell.

"So it's like this, spunky little Amy. In here you come selling your pretty pieces, just to get you enough money to enter your pony in the Ladies Mile Race in May. A pony is too small for a big race meeting like that. You will fin…"

Amy snapped back from her thoughts.

"But…Well he's a big pony. He's fourteen two hands. If you put bigger shoes on him, like the shoes with little heels that you see the hunters with, he would stand over fourteen two. And he runs so fast. He even runs faster up hill than anywhere."

"So you run him a lot do you?"

"Oh yes, almost every afternoon after school. We run the hills behind the Meadowbank. He loves the hills and the bush is full of creeks and fallen logs, he jumps them all." Her eyes shone with excitement. And her new friend looked at her with a long, studied look.

"There will be some big horses in the Ladies race. Some of those horsewomen are tough, why those girls, they have been riding, hunting and racing long before you and your pony cut teeth."

Amy suddenly remembered she was wasting precious time. She had only an hour after school before she had to be home. She began to gather up the three pieces and put them back in the paper bag it had been so nice talking to him, but she had to keep going.

"Now hold on! Hold on young lady. You and I still have some unfinished business."

"But I have to be home by four-thirty. It has been very nice talking to you." Amy was suddenly ready to leave.

"Tell me. How much money do you need to enter your pony in this race?"

Amy pulled her school bag back on.

"The entry fee is ten shillings. I need to get it by next Thursday, or I will miss out."

"Right then. Let's you and me make a deal then."

"A deal. What is a deal?"

"Why; it's an agreement between two parties. Gentlemen shake hands on a deal and it becomes an honourable bond. Each party keeps to the agreement."

"Is that why people say – your word is your bond?"

"Yes. And I want to make a deal with you. I will give you ten shillings for your pieces." He held up his hand to stop her from talking. "But! When you win the Ladies Mile Race at Ellerslie, you will then return here, pay me back the ten shillings and I will return to you these very pretty pieces."

Amy was stunned. She just stood there with her mouth open. Her eyes were big with his offer. His new friend grinned his biggest grin, reaching his hand toward her over the counter, she placed her own small hand in his in a still not yet familiar handshake.

"Reggie Kennett's the name, Amy. Reginald Frederick Johnstone Kennett at your service. Now Amy, do we have a deal!"

CHAPTER 7

AMY LAY IN her bed and gazed out on the tree tops. There was no moon and the wind was blowing strongly, bending the trees. The rustling sounds they made were a sweet background music to the warmth of the bed. She wanted to shout. Had wanted to shout as she ran home. Didn't really feel like running, more like flying than running. The ten shilling note sat on her dressing table, anchored there by her hairbrush. Tomorrow she would take it to the Racecourse and buy the entry ticket. Her toes curled up just thinking about it. Oh cripes. Oh thank you God. I don't know how you pulled that off for me, but, well, was He not great? I will have to train Friska hard, he is fit now, but there is a lot of work to do.

The second visit to the race course was easy. This time she knew where to go and Vic had smiled with her, enjoying her delight at being able to purchase her race entry ticket. Over the following weeks, Amy rode Friska every afternoon after school. Once out of site of the house and the village, they would gallop across the hills. The love to run and the strength needed to do so built up in Friska a little more each day. Amy would walk him home for the last mile to cool him down as the gallops left his coat wet with sweat. Back at the shed she would hose him lightly and rub him down. She ran him in the rain also, dodging her mother before a wet workout to avoid the chance of being kept back, she needed to work in both the rain and the shine. Once worked and fed she would lean on the gate and watch him. We can do it, can't we? Yes, we can... I really think so!

*   *   *

The old Maori woman stood up and rubbed her stiff hip. She gave it a wriggle as if to put it back into its rightful place. 'Eh! 'She muttered to herself, 'this being a kuia ain't such a good idea, too bad the great creator hadn't made th' humans to be forever young. But what's the good of that then. All fullas haffta make it to Reinga sometime. Guess that y'cant hurry it or slow it down. It's gonna do its thing whatever y'reckon.' Huia gathered firewood from the rough tin shelter behind her shack. 'Just as well th' mokupuna was with her,' she mused, 'bless his shining heart, can't get better than her Joe, and did y'ever hear any boy sing like her Joe? Nah, eh, outshines th' Tui does Joe when he sings.'

Her body might be cracking up but her ears were as sharp as ever. She suddenly stopped her muttering, standing still, her aches forgotten. Sounds of thumps and sticks cracking down by the creek, someone or something was coming, coming fast and carelessly, that was for certain... no one came this way, just her mokupuna Joe when he came home from school. Her ears turned themselves sharp, listening close and carefully, then, quietly she felt the presence, eh, it made a small smile in her face.

"Huh, eh! That be you Amy, you and your pony. Oi! C'min 'ere... Hey you Amy! Over here!" Huia dropped the armful of wood and picked up her tall walking stick.

Amy could hear Huia calling and she urged Friska towards the sound and he happily picked his way amongst the familiar trees. The old woman came into sight waving her stick. Amy well knew Huia's stick, had been shown it once before in earlier, shared moments of what, for most Maori, were somewhat rare, special, and sacred. At the time, Amy had known that she had been given a special gift by the old kuia, had been shown the intricate carvings on the stick each curving, an exquisite pattern carved in and around the shining, dark wood, each curve and

38

curl told some story of old Huia's life and of her ancestry. Maori put great faith and mana into their ancestors, and the stories of great battles, or of great love, were woven together in carvings and songs. Now that same stick was hitting at the sky in sharp gestures.

"Oi! Amy!" Old Huia called again, "Cum 'ere!"

Amy loved the brown old lady. Most of the local people gave her a wide berth, keeping away and calling her 'Huia, Huia, crazy old kuia', but Amy had learned long ago that these were only tall tales. Old Huia encouraged them to think her crazy so that they would stay away and leave her in peace. Huia was small and bent, a moko decorated her wrinkled chin, placed there long ago when tradition and a rangatira birth had insisted that she receive the purple design. Etched forever into her skin it looked a natural part of her. Huia's grandson Joe lived with her and went to Amy's school. Joe knew, as Amy also knew, that Huia had powers that the pakeha would never understand. It was old, early Maori stuff like Tohungas and spirits. Amy knew and respected the powers, whatever they were, ever since Huia had picked her up from out of the creek when she had taken a bad fall from Friska. Huia had taken her into her dirt floor shack and helped her. 'A drunk head' Huia had called it, 'half knocked out from that old tree stump y' hit wi' y' head wi' flyin' through th' air.' The Maori concoctions Amy sipped, although they tasted ghastly, had soothed away the pain.

"Eh! Y' look like 'n angel sittin up there." Huia grinned a toothless grin up at Amy as she eased Friska over towards the rough yard. "C'min 'ave a cuppa tea wi' 'n old woman." Huia grinned even wider.

"Is Joe home?"

"Nah. He's off with his mates eelin' at th' mill wheel pond."

They both burst into laughing. It's what you did with Huia. Her Maori laugh seemed to come up from her toes, like a long delicious chuckle that ran slowly all the way up through her bent old body and then straightening her torso slightly, finally escaped in infectious sound through the gap in her face, only to return again to her toes for a repeat performance…

Far back in the wooded hills, hidden from the world, Huia lived in a corrugated iron shack. Inside the only room was small and dark, with a floor of pressed dirt. The cooking area was a corrugated iron fire place with an iron bar that balanced on an odd assortment of bricks. Iron hooks hung from the bar a heavy camp oven loaded with the evenings stew hanging from it. A collection of chaff sacks sewn together separated the sleeping area, where crude bunks made of tea tree poles ran the length of the walls. Wild fern, gathered from nearby dried and tied thickly together, made warm clean, easily replaced mattresses. Huia picked up the battered water kettle and joined by Amy, they wandered out to the creek that ran beside the house, filling the kettle with the clear water. The creek was her water supply and all of the washing was done in it. Amy watched as Huia hung the water kettle on the low hook, and placing a handful of dried twigs over the smouldering embers, she blew the fire to life.

"Eh!" she chuckled. "Joe, he's good at catching eels. Give us a good dinner eh. D' y' like eels Amy?"

"Oh no Huia. No. They are so slippery and slimy. I don't even like poking them with a stick when you have them swimming in the bucket."

Once again they both burst out laughing.

"Slimy eh! Slippery eh! You pakeha don't know what yer missin'. heh heh. There ain' nothing like a good stewed eel t' put some muscle on yer skinny bones."

"My bones are fine just as they are. Skinny am I. Well I shall need to be before long." Amy had not meant to say it but it just slipped out. It must have been the laughing it just made things happen, even when you did not want them to. Amy crossed her fingers and sat on them. Oh cripes, she said in her head, please God, don't let her have heard that.

Too late. Her sharp ears missed nothing and her sense perception also was acute, Huia picked it up at once. She looked silently at Amy for what seemed a long time. Laughter was one thing but silence, especially this silence, was like talking without making any sound.

"Hmm. You up to somethin' eh. You sittin' on hands. You not tell yer Father eh. What y' up to girl? It's not anytin' like you to be hidin' stuff, you the open, honest one, it not sit good wi you. Y' got it writtin' all over you!"

Amy sighed. Oh cripes and crikey, she should not have come in. Should have waved and ridden on. Just because Huia did not have many, or any, visitors, Amy did not need to be the only one. She should have gone on working Friska, after all the race was now only three weeks away. How stupid can you get, she told herself.

Huia took a stained clay pipe from the cracked cup on the fireplace hearth. Tapping it upside down against the hearth, emptying its spent remains, she then silently loaded tobacco from a yellow, 'Old Gold' tin, and pressed it down into the small pipe bowl. It was an uncomfortable silence, sharpened by the now gone laughter. She took up a long, dry twig and held it over the flame, once alight, she placed it over the pipe bowl, pressing the tobacco down with a horny thumb and drawing air in through the tobacco wad with a long, satisfying intake of breath. The tobacco glowed red as she pulled in another breath, making sure that the light had caught and would hold, it sent a pungent smell into the small room.

Sitting easily on the rough, stone hearth, her feet drawn up under her long, faded, black skirt and hugging her skinny knees, the old woman puffed contentedly.

"You not tell 'im eh. Yer Dad. Y'got somethin' comin' up and he won't like it. But it won't matter. The whole hidden stuff will blow over, 'cause its writtn' in you. Easy for anyone t' see. So what y plannin'? Some scheme or other that y can't share wt anyone. S' hard when yer can't share, but wi' you it int gonna matter."

Once again they both became silent, the only sound was the hissing of the water in the kettle as it began to boil, and the saliva gurgle in the old Kuia's pipe as she puffed away.

Once the Kuia had made the tea and they had moved out to sit on the fallen log that served as an outdoor couch, Me patio, Huia called it. The tall trees by the shack made an ideal sheltered area, it was all so comfortable and easy sitting there, Amy found that the words began to simply tumble from her. She told the old Maori everything. How her father had never actually said that NO she could not ride, how she came to have the entry money, how well Friska was strengthening up with the after school training, and how she felt that it was right to do this. In fact she had to do it.

"Eh. So y' didn't lie to y' Dad, Y' just didn't tell th' whole story. Eh. Well lemme see… Hmmm…" Huia sucked again on her pipe, unmindful of it having gone out. She gazed out over the tree tops. The small creek sang running over its stones, and a quiet breeze lazily moved the top leaves, and came weaving in a warm flow, amongst the lower trunks, stroking gently across Amy's arms. A contented, steady munching came from Friska, as he enjoyed the new grass growing under the trees. Amy leaned back and relaxed. It was such a relief to have put all that had happened in the last few weeks into words and to share them with another. She had not noticed how much keeping a secret could build up inside, and now, letting it all out in words, and who better than old Huia, was like a long, cool drink on the hottest day.

"Well girl," Huia said at last. "Let's hava look n see what th' tea leaves have to say. Here, gimmi yer cup."

Amy handed over the tin mug, not fooled for one moment at the suggestion of reading the tea leaves, she knew that whatever the old one had to say, it would be coming from another place and not from the leaf residue in an empty tin mug.

"Eh. Heh heh heh. Ah heh heh heh." The chuckles started again. "Oh it 'd be good t' be there. Heh heh." Her toothless grin got wider. "Well m' angel, how d' yer feel about th' race commin' up, 'n how does yer pony feel?

Amy was surprised by the question. "Well actually I feel very very good about it. I did from the start, and not telling my Dad, well I just couldn't help it. I could not even tell my best friend Pammy. She would have not understood and would have tried hard to talk me out of the whole thing. She was dead against me riding in the race, and I thought it would really only happen if I kept it to myself. A secret. As for Friska, we have been training hard and he just gets fitter and faster."

"He look pretty small next to them big thoroughbreds. Them horses take one stride to his two."

"He's fourteen two hands high," said Amy defensively. "Oh Huia, I really think that he can outrun them and I have stopped eating my Mum's scones and sandwiches…"

"Eh. Heh heh, yer tink it'll make yer lighter. He heh heh… Yer already pretty light. Y' know girl, y' got good guidance. It sokay fer you to be doin' this. It sokay. Y' pony he tough and fast and who knows what th' day will bring. But I tell y' what. You git yerself down to that Andy Anderson. He is a top un for the shoeing, and y' git him to put on light running shoes. Ones with' little heels on 'em. Y've seen em in the shows, so y' get in and have him do it. And don't fergit th' heels. He knows how t' do it."

"B-but Huia, how do you know so much about horses and shoeing?"

"Eh. Heh he heh," she chuckled again, pointing her empty clay pipe at Amy. "Yer young fullas always tink we older uns git born old."

CHAPTER 8

Every afternoon Amy rode Friska over the hills. Once out of sight, they galloped, pretending that they were racing. Building up speed. Building up muscle. Fast along the track by the river bank, then up the steep slope, pushing the willing pony ever faster towards the top of the hills, jumping whatever came across their path; fallen logs, ditches and wide streams. As the pony's judgement, already acute, increased, so did their confidence in each other. Amy rode low in the saddle. Another of Huia's tips.

"Ride like you ride. Don't try and be like the others. Those fullas on race horses all ride high up. That not for you." She could still hear Huia's words - "you ride like you ride. You already a part of th' horse".

That week she took Friska to the farrier to have the new light racing shoes fitted. Her father, accustomed to having the pony shod when needed, had not questioned her request for new shoes. Fortunately, the farrier also had not asked why she wanted light shoes with heels. The heels were small extensions to the shoes and worn only on the hind hooves. Amy loved to watch the farrier fit the pony with new shoes, all that banging and clanging when the iron horse shoe, glowing red from the forge, was beaten into the right shape for the horse by rough, skilled hands. Now as Friska ran up the hills the small heels gave him the extra grip in the soft ground.

As she usually did, Amy worked Friska that afternoon after school. Amy walked Friska the last mile home, not that he wanted to walk, excited and fit, he danced and he pranced, tossing his head up and down, working against her light fingers as she steadied him with the reins. He needed to be cooled down after so much running. Once back in the home yard, Amy watered and fed him, grooming and crooning to him as she worked.

"We can do this together, Friska. We can do this. We can do this."

Once more she sat in the hay and watched him, grabbing a few extra moments before she needed to return to the house, opening the gate from the yard so the pony could move back into his paddock, once his chaff and oats were eaten. Later, lying in her bed, she gazed out through the open window at the stars. It was a clear, crisp night. A cricket was chirping his long, unending song from somewhere nearby. Those crickets can get pretty rowdy, she thought as she snuggled into the warm bed. Why was it that the stars seemed bigger and brighter tonight? What were they anyway? Were there other worlds like this one? At school they learned about Saturn, Mars and Jupiter, all part they were told, of our solar system. But what was beyond that? There were too many stars to count. There had to be other worlds it just made sense that there would be. Surely God would not limit His creation to just one world?

Her mind was too full and too busy for sleep. Climbing out of bed, she folded her arms onto the window sill, the warm wood dug into her waist as she leaned out toward the night. There was no breeze at all and the tall trees across the lawn stood in friendly silence. The night smells were dense with different perfumes, as grass, trees and flowers mixed themselves together. She listened for the sounds as the carousing cricket took time off from its piercing song. A dog barked in the distance, echoing softly and the contented pull of grass, followed by its easily heard munching, came from the house cow through the nearby fence.

Amy took in a long breath. It came out again as a long, deep sigh. I love it she thought. How beautiful it all is. If this is what God can do, what else can He do? Do we know half, or any of it. Those science classes at school, with the dividing of amoebas and stuff. And now all of this new stuff they have been giving us about Darwin and the theory of evolution. What makes him, this Darwin, right? Is it just what he thinks and not what anyone else thinks? Then how come is it that donkeys do not progress over time into horses, let alone zebras? Or why don't snakes evolve into eels or vice a versa. He says that apes evolved into humans? Nah. What makes him right? Who says he is right? I just cannot see that it is anything other than an opinion. Opinions? What are they? Where do thoughts come from? Actually, just what is a thought? Here I am thinking that I can win a race up a long hill and over many fences and what is it that makes me think that? It is not all just thinking, I can feel it, here, somewhere here in the middle of myself, where nothing goes but me, and where, for reasons that I really can't understand, is a knowing? Yep, it's just a knowing.

CHAPTER 9

Misty rain settled over the creek, hiding the distant valley and the one tree hill from site. Joe Sigley rubbed his leg, an unthinking motion that did little to ease the dull pain the Great War had left him with, the dampness always seemed to increase the pain, bringing with it the memories that came crowding in, catching him off guard with their intensity. He shrugged them away as he always did, not allowing his mind to retain the thoughts. Throwing them out of his head and replacing them by studying his surroundings. A discipline he had formed for himself over the years.

He had acquired his small farm as a returned serviceman, "re-habs" they called them. Assisted by the Government, the soldiers returning from the war had been given allotments, small farms to re-habilitate them in their return to civilian life. Joe leaned on the gate. Having never been a smoker, unlike so many of his mates, he pulled a long blade of grass, chewing it softly as his gaze wandered over the farm. It looked like a park, peeping out as the mist began to clear. Wide green paddocks, not a weed to be seen, stretched around him. The batten and wire fences, taut and strong, marched like soldiers on parade, stretching before him. Joe had purchased his neighbour's re-hab allotment five years earlier. He had watched his neighbour struggle hard. The Government, making these seemingly generous offers, had made the acreage much too small to be economically viable and many of the returned men had broken their hearts trying to gain enough of a livelihood, milking small herds of cows. The money earned was not enough and anything extra was taken away, in their efforts to bring the land into greater production. Joe and his family would not have survived had he not been able to buy out his neighbour and increase his acreage.

A sudden flash movement in the distance made Joe glance up, screwing up his eyes to see across the green space to the road from the village. Tom ran into sight. He sped along the road and didn't stop at the farm gate but leapt over it in one fluid movement, with one hand on the top rail as he did so. Joe watched him as he slowed down to a jog once he came closer to the house.

The boy is nearly a man, he mused, and runs faster than ever. Certainly loves to run. He is the one to apply himself, not like his brother William. Joe sighed as he thought of William. Could he leave him the farm one day? Although brothers, the two boys had completely different natures. Tom so easy going but William could be mean. He shook his head. He did not want to look at the truth, but then decided he must. He admitted in his thoughts; yes, William had a mean streak. He was grateful that his only daughter Janet was older than the boys. At eighteen she was already employed at the local school. A teacher's assistant they called it. Preparation for entering training as a teacher next year. Not much else for a young girl to do, mused Joe, go nursing or teaching, or maybe a typist, how much more choice there was for the boys.

Tom ran in the door. He gave his mother a quick hug as she turned to greet him, then snatching up a biscuit from the laden table, headed for the bedroom, only to turn back as his sister Janet, sitting curled up in the easy chair studying an open magazine, called to him.

"Your clothes are wet with sweat Tom. Honestly, do you have to get so sweaty?"

He reached over and grabbed her magazine, dancing around the floor with it pretending to look at the pictures.

"Ooh and YOU my dear! Oh look, what a jolly old outfit this is, Oh my, but look at this, and this." He waved the pages away as she tried to reach for them, holding them high out of reach with his long arms.

"YOU PIG TOM! GIVE IT BACK!" Janet grabbed his shirt, pulling it from his waist. Tom ran out of the door and around the house, with Janet charging after him. Their mother, used to their antics, ignored them. Joe came up the path just as Janet careered around the corner bowling straight into him.

"Ouch. Oh, sorry Dad." she gasped.

"TOM." Joe bellowed, "Stop teasing your sister. Come on, give her back her book. I have plenty for you to do with all that energy. Get some work gear on, we have hay to feed out to the cows."

Tom grinned, folded up the magazine and held it out to Janet, then, just as she reached for it, he snatched it back, and picking her up, carried both girl and magazine over his shoulder, squealing and kicking, back into the kitchen, placing both gently back in the chair where they had been moments before.

Pulling on his work clothes, Tom headed into the yard. He brought the horse from the home paddock and harnessed it to the sled, glad to be giving his father a break. Tom bought both horse and sled through the gateway to the hay barn. Skilfully he turned the horse around in the small space inside the barn, and began to load the sled using a pitchfork, plunging it into the stack of hay and swinging it into a neat pile on to the sled. It would take two sled loads to feed the twenty breeding cows. Thank goodness, he thought, his old man raised breeding cows and was not in dairy. Some of his school friends lived on dairy farms. Many of their herds were between ten and twenty cows, and to Tom, it seemed that the farm children did most of the milking. Milking by hand was a tough job. His mate Terry was always made to milk the cows, and he was often late for school. Terry and his brother and sisters had to bring in the cows at five each morning, and were never able to stay and play any games after school. Just straight home for the evening milking. Tom loathed to see them so burdened. Terry's hands had deep cracks in the skin from the cold mornings and the milking.

Together Joe and Tom guided the loaded sled out to the paddock, and forked the loose hay on to the ground for the cows to eat. They worked in companionable silence. When all was done, they sat side by side on the sled.

"You know Tom," Joe began softly. "They have formed an Athletic Club in Newmarket. I hear that they use a new Stadium on the hill above the railway track. Built rows of seats into the hill for a grandstand. Lots of building going on at the moment, now that the slump seems to be over, and thank God for that. How would it be if you joined the Athletic Club. I understand, from what I have read in the paper, they meet every Saturday."

"Athletic Club Dad? You mean that they run races? I dunno. I never thought about it."

"Well maybe you should. You seem to like to run, and you have quite a turn of speed. A boy needs something more than just helping his Dad on the farm and going to school, help him get a wider look at life."

Tom gazed at the cows munching the fresh hay. He was surprised at his father's words. He had never thought of running races, except at the school sports day, and that was only once a year. This was a new thought. What if he could run with other athletes every week. A small butterfly started to fly around in his stomach, as the idea began to take hold.

"Would I walk in to Newmarket? It is not all that far. How would I find the stadium. And gosh Dad, who would I talk to?"

"I reckon we could go in together for a time. Get you to know the place, and find your way around. We could take the train, it's only ten minutes by train to Newmarket."

Tom laughed, suddenly excited.

"One day I will buy us a car."

"Ah, there are more of them on the road every day. Smelly noisy things. Give me a horse any day."

"You know Dad, I really think that I would like to take a crack at that."

Joe felt twinges of satisfaction as he walked home, watching Tom ride on the sled ahead of him, bringing the horse back towards the barn. The feeling disappeared fast, as he thought of William. Now if he could only think up something that would bring some positive direction for William. He shook his head, puzzling, searching for ideas. But none came.

CHAPTER 10

THE HOT WEATHER continued into May. It was only ten days until the race day and Amy could think of little else. She and Pammy returned to their classroom as the headmaster rang the school bell, bringing all the pupils in from their lunchtime break. Everyone was hot and breathless from their games as they clattered into the desks and the classroom was cool and dark after the bright sunlight. All the desks were double, each seating two pupils. The two girls sat together, with Mokupuna Joe and Tom seated behind them. Pammy was wearing a long white sash around her waist that looked pretty against her blue dress, but after all of their running around the playground during the break, both dress and sash sat crazily askew. Amy gave her a teasing poke as they scrambled into their seats.

"You're all crooked."

"And look who's talking. Have you started a new fashion of shirts out over skirts. Tuck yourself in Amy."

"Oh Okay," said Amy doing so. "But cripes, does it have to be History again?" She fiddled with her pens, placing them in the grooves that ran along top of the desk, checking that her inkwell, in its small hole on the right, held plenty of ink, and straightening her, already straight, ruler. Oh God, she muttered to herself, I really hate History, all those dates and names and places. What use is it all going to be? She wriggled into her seat as the afternoon sun shone in through the high window, making it hard to concentrate as the headmaster pointed out the events on the blackboard with his cane.

Tom was feeling hot and dozy. Beside him, Mokupuna Joe began to play with the end of Pammy's sash, that trailed over the seat in front of him. Pammy tugged back the sash and whispered, "Quit it."

Joe held on, as she turned back to the front. He grinned to himself as the headmaster droned on. Tom gave him a nudge as Joe began to dip the end of her sash into the inkwell on his desk. The end of the white sash was soon holding a deep blue ink splodge. Unknowing, Pammy tried to tug her sash back but the grinning Joe held on.

"Let go," she muttered. "Come on Joe, dammit." She kept her eyes to the front, not wanting to attract the headmaster's attention.

"Sit still!" whispered Amy, as Pammy wriggled around.

"I can't… It's Joe, he…"

Amy jumped up, grabbing her ruler. She turned and whacked Joe over his fingers. "Dammit Joe. Let go!"

"Ouch!" Joe rubbed his fingers.

Tom snatched Amy's ruler from her hand and held it out of her reach.

"STOP AT ONCE!" Mr. Bright the headmaster bellowed at them, whacking his cane, with a great bang, on the front of his desk. "JUST WHAT DO YOU THINK YOU ARE DOING AMY!"

"Er… Sorry Sir. Um… Well I just…"

"It was Joe!" accused Pammy.

"No Sir. Er… My fault." Amy said weakly.

"Not her Sir," called Tom, still holding Amy's ruler.

The headmaster glared at them all, reading with experienced accuracy the whole episode.

"Joe! Tom! OUT! You will wait for me in the corridor."

"But Sir…"

"OUT! Not another word!" The headmaster pointed to the door with his cane. Sheepishly, Tom and Joe filed out of the room.

"All right class. You will open your books to page forty three, and I want you to write up the description at the end of the chapter that concludes the last half hour of this lesson. I expect you to hand those written papers to me when I return." He marched from the room, following the two boys.

"They are gonna get the cane," the sing song words of Ben Hartley from across the room.

"Don't be so stupid Ben. Of course they won't be caned," countered Amy. "They did not behave badly enough for that kind of punishment."

"Well hoity toity to you too, smart Miss Amy," taunted Ben. "You betcha they will get caned all right, th' head was already pretty mad at all of the lack of attention."

Amy glared at him. Nah. They would not get caned, would they? She hated the thought. Often the boys in the small school were caned for misbehaviour. The headmaster had a silent policy that he would punish the boys in the accepted way, but he would never strike a girl. Their punishment would have to be of a different kind. Usually the girls were kept in after school.

Amy glared again at Ben, then she jumped to her feet and ran from the classroom. Outside, at the end of the long, dark corridor, Joe and Tom stood before the headmaster, the body language the small group gave off was unmistakable. It said it all. The two boys were standing as if ready for the caning and the headmaster, as if pushing himself to his task, was bending his cane as he glared at them.

Amy paused, taking in the scene, then she strode up to the group and placed herself between the teacher and the two boys.

"And what is this may I ask?" barked the headmaster.

"Please! It is not their fault. It is all my fault. I just suddenly got impatient and turned and wacked Joe's fingers with my ruler. I am sorry Sir, but you really can't punish them when it is not their fault. If you cane them, you will have to cane me first." Amy was angry at such an injustice. She stood as tall as she could, as if guarding Tom and Joe, daring the teacher to strike her.

There was a stunned silence. All you could hear was the breathing of the four standing at the end of the corridor. The tension between them mounted as, surprised and unsure, the headmaster studied the angry girl. Just as suddenly, he smiled to himself.

"So it is your fault Amy? And not these two?"

"You will have to cane me first Sir. It really was all my fault."

The fair-minded man turned and laid the cane on the chair behind him. Turning back, he looked at all three, the defiant girl and the two boys, all trying hard to look very serious.

"Very well Amy, I shall accept your defence. You will write me one hundred lines. They will be handed in after school today. You will write, 'I shall listen and attend' on every line. Now, you will all return to the classroom, and I will not hear another word from any of you. Is that clear!"

"Yes Sir," muttered all three in unison. Relieved, they turned and walked back into the room.

Their classmates suddenly became active, picking up pens and opening books, breaking the silence that had them listening to every word coming from outside the room.

A few minutes later Tom passed Amy a screwed up note, unfolding it under her desk it read, "Thanks Champ - we will help you write the lines." She hid her hand behind her back and gave him an "OK" sign.

CHAPTER 11

It was Thursday. In two days time it would be the May Ellerslie Races. Amy lay in her bed feeling the butterflies in her stomach begin to rise at the thought. She had to get up. Had to make the day into a normal day. Go to school, talk and laugh and play, as if there was nothing out of the ordinary happening. She thought of Friska in his paddock, I will rest him up for the next two days, she thought to herself, I have been working him hard for the past five weeks, and a couple of light days will have him jumping out of his skin. She crossed her fingers and folded them over her chest. Please, she whispered, looking up to an unseen God, I know You hear me, You are always there, You always guide me, so please, let nothing happen to stop us being in the race, please make it all right with my Dad. Oh, if I never asked You for anything again, I ask You for this. Make Saturday fine and sunny. Make it OK for Friska and me…

The next two days were the longest days of Amy's life. The hours seemed to drag endlessly on, as both school and home life, took on an unreal quality. She was walking around in a half dream. The normal chatter of her mother and father, as well as trying to share at school with her friends, felt like walking waste high in the sea, dragging every step.

"What's the matter with you Amy. You're like a zombie. You haven't heard a word I've said. We haven't done ice-creams for weeks! Can you come with me? Aw… come on Amy."

"Okay Pammy. Yes, you're right. We haven't been into the village for weeks. Sorry. I have been kind of tied up." Amy sighed with relief, she had planned not to run Friska anyway, the training programme had kept her away from her friend, she let Pammy take over.

"What have you been so tied up with? It's not like you to get all secretive on us."

"Gosh. S'pose I have been really. Sorry, just seem to have had heaps of extra stuff to do lately."

Pammy shrugged, accepting Amy's feeble explanation.

"Look. It's Joe and Tom." She waved to them and the two boys stopped and waited for them to catch up. A soft, unspoken bond had developed following the 'un-caning' episode. Amy had been able to hand in her hundred lines early, as both boys had shared the boring task, each writing a portion in the afternoon break.

"Whatcha doing with the weekend?" Tom asked as they walked on together.

"Ha, me?" Joe answered first. "I want to help my kuia in the morning. Goin' to cut fresh fern, it's just the right time of year for the fern. Reckon I'll get some good raupo while I am at it, put it on the floor for the winter and warm the place up. After that? Well I reckon I will go and take a look at the Ellerslie races."

Amy tripped over her own feet and stumbled on the pavement.

"G-G-Go to the races?"

"Yep, my kuia used to ride in the races. They had 'em out on the beach at Waiuku. Yep. Heaps of the Maori girls would ride against the men. Yep, my kuia knows lots about the races."

"Not me" said Tom, and again Amy heaved a quiet sigh of relief. "I'm taking a look at the new athletic stadium they built in Newmarket. Going in there with my Dad on Saturday morning." He carefully did not add, that he would be running there.

"I think I'll just muck around at home," Amy crossed her fingers and mumbled, hoping that no one would ask her any questions. "Maybe take my pony Friska for a ride over Dalebrooks farm and out to the river."

Tom looked at her, slightly puzzled, it was easy to see that she was not being all that honest.

Pammy broke the spell.

"Not me, I'm off to Avondale. My cousins are having a big party and our whole family are going. Gonna take the train to Newmarket and then change to the northern line train to Avondale and go to their house for a big family lunch. It is my Uncles' fortieth birthday and there will be about thirty of us, I'm really looking forward to it we just have so much fun together."

Thirty of them, thought Amy later as she brushed Friska and gave him his feed box. As an only child with no cousins or family in the country, she could not imagine being among thirty cousins, all of her family were back in England. She brushed Friska slowly, savouring the smell of him. He pushed his ears forward as she whispered to him, snorting gently down his nose, not caring what she said, but loving it in the way horses do. Amy ran her hands down his legs, feeling for any lumps or bumps, her sensitive fingers searching for any spots of heat that would indicate a sprain or injury. Gratefully she found none.

"Races on Saturday, Amy." Her father pushed his chair back from the dining table as her mother gathered up the empty plates. "Have y' got y' best dress ready? We'll be along there by ten. May as well enjoy the day and get there before the main crowd. We can find ourselves a good spot in the stands and it will be all over by two thirty, these races always end early, it gives the farmers time to get home and milk their herds."

Oh no. She crossed her fingers and sat on them.

Her mother smiled.

"Y' can wear that new green dress, it's warm enough. Not too cold yet for short sleeves and it's so pretty why it makes your eyes twice the colour they are and how nice it is to wear a new dress."

"Oh. Oh, Daddy. If it is all right, I really don't want to go to the races that morning." How was she going to get out of it without telling an outright lie. Her mind raced around, looking for a way out. What to do. What to say. Please', she said inside herself, help me.

"Daddy, Mokupuna Joe is gathering fern and raupo on Saturday morning."

"Do you want to give him a hand? Is that it? He's a good boy that Joe. Really looks after his old grandmother the kuia. Well I dunno how much I want you running around alone while we are at the races. What d' y' think Katie?" He looked at his wife.

Amy squeezed her fingers tighter. She wanted to close her eyes, but knew that would give her away so she stared at one of the blue squares on the gingham table cloth, hardly breathing.

Katie looked at her daughter and pondered the question. She trusted Amy. Trusted her completely. Katie knew that she was up to something, she had been for weeks, but whatever it was it was not a bad thing, she felt her trust and confidence in her daughter rise, yes, she would be all right.

"Let her choose." she responded gently. "We can enjoy the races, it will be fine. Perhaps, Amy, you would like us to put a small bet on one of the horses for you. That would be a good idea as there are plenty running, let's see now, what colour horse shall I back for you? Or maybe you would rather choose th' jockey's colours." Katie did not miss the silent sigh of relief that Amy released at her words.

"Choose a horse on its colours? What?" Doug could not believe how truly stupid that would be. "You can't be serious!"

"Sure we can," laughed his wife, knowing she had transferred all pressure from Amy. "And win we will. You just see if we don't!"

CHAPTER 12

SATURDAY CAME. AMY watched her parents as they walked from the house, down the driveway heading for the racetrack. Her father looked so handsome in his dark grey suit and tie, his grey felt hat straight and tidy on his head, her sweet mother in a wide navy straw hat and blue dress, they looked so unusually elegant when compared to their usual working clothes. Her mother turned and waved as they passed out of sight down the road.

Amy leapt into gear. It was nine o'clock. She had brought Friska into the yard at six, keeping him from eating any grass, just as Huia had told her. Can't run on a full stomach, she had said. Sleep had not come easily for Amy in the night, leaving her tossing and turning in her bed, climbing out to look from her window, praying to her silent God to please, help her through, trying again to sleep only to toss and turn until her sheet was in one big knot. She had finally fallen asleep, waking fretfully at quarter to six and jumping from her bed to bring in the pony.

With her parents gone she climbed into her jodhpurs and boots, she tucked in her white blouse and put a hair band in her hair, fastening it with hair clips, making sure that it would remain in place, not wanting any hair in her eyes when she lest expected. By nine-thirty she and Friska were out of the gate and on the road, the race track was an easy ten minute ride and the Ladies Mile Race was due to start at eleven. There was no time for any delays. Her stomach felt as if it had moved tightly against her backbone, as Friska trotted along at an easy pace, the feelings grew stronger as if leaving her backbone to climb up into her throat, her stomach had misplaced itself inside her body, increasing in tightness as they neared the race course. Sensing her fear and excitement, as the sounds from the race course grew louder, Friska began to dance and play up. He tossed his head, fighting the soft restraint of her fingers on the reins, skipping sideways, then prancing in a circle. Amy forgot her mounting fear, using all her will to calm him. The pony resisted, and standing on his hind legs, spun around wanting to run. Moving with him, Amy put her hand on his neck, it was covered in nervous sweat from his excitement.

"It's okay," she whispered. "Take it easy boy. That's better. Yes, there are horses everywhere. S'okay. You'll get your run, there now s'okay." She crooned him into a quieter mood as they passed in through the heavy iron gates. She reigned Friska in wondering which way to go, there were people everywhere. The pony put his head down, snorting at the ground, and she continued to calm him as she stood up high in her stirrups looking around, hoping to spot a familiar face.

*   *   *

Huia rose in the dark. It would soon be daylight. She dressed in her long black skirt and shirt and tied a wide, black scarf low over her head, covering her white hair from sight. Taking her tall, carved stick, she stood for several moments in the open doorway and holding the knob on the end of the stick against her forehead, she said a silent karakia to the spirits of the morning, sending life force flowing through from her forehead and into the stick.

Huia crossed the creek and took a short, narrow path among the fern, heading into the dense bush that grew at the back of her shack. She walked on, looking for what she wanted and gave a satisfied grunt when she spotted the low punga tree. The punga frond was easily reached, it grew from the centre of the low tree in a perfect curl, a "koru" the Maori called it, a beautiful, brown centre curving up from the plant like a large, curled question mark. Taking a pocket knife from her belt, Huia bowed her head to the plant, asking for its permission to take the 'koru', she then cut the tall frond cleanly through and holding it before her walked on into the bush. The darkness had become tinged with grey light making the path easy to follow as she continued on to a small clearing beneath a giant, wide puriri tree where four stones were placed in a small square on the ground. Quietly the old woman turned to face the rising sun. The stones marked the four earth compass points north, south, east and west. A large, flat stone held its place in the centre. Carefully Huia stepped onto the centre stone. She began to draw a circle in the dirt with her stick, taking it around the outside of the stones, as she chanted a quiet karakia, turning with the stick as it encompassed the four stones, then changing position she placed her hands on the end of the stick shaft concentrating on watching the life force flow through her hands and she raised it up and pointed the knob towards the rising sun. She remained, perfectly still, in that position for many moments, letting the knob on the end of the stick absorb the life-giving rays of the early sun. Calling the one great father of all the universe to send her his spirits of speed and strength, to bring them to work for her this day. She continued her karakia for many long moments then, lowering the stick she carefully placed the ponga frond on the flat stone in the centre of the circle making sure the line of the curl flowed in the direction from west to east, the way a pakeha clock would turn the universal left to right direction, the positive flow of the universe, that will bring harmony and joy. Placing it the wrong way would bring disintegration and scattering.

Back in her shack, still fresh with the early morning, the kuia brought her fire to life and set the kettle over the flames. She settled down to wait and would eat nothing until after the event, but a cup of tea would go down well. She reached for her clay pipe and tapped it against the hearth stones, pushing a plug of tobacco into the bowl from the "Old Gold" tin. After lighting the pipe with her usual ceremony, she quietly puffed away, rocking gently back and forth, knowing that the spirits she had engaged were waiting for the time when she would need them.

* * *

"Amy, Amy! Over here." Having begun to feel quite lost, Amy

felt relief flood through her as the familiar thick, short figure of Vic appeared through a large cluster of horses.

"I have a spot for you over here, you're only just in time, y' have to be in th' race paddock in thirty minutes. What kept you? You have to register. Here, let me hold your horse. Y' have to get y' number from the stewards' room over there." He gestured towards the rear of the large grandstand. "Y' need to hurry. G'wan. Go." Vic took Friska's reins as Amy did as he said. She could not tell him that she did not want to be seen, and so had cut the time short. Vic held Friska steady; his voice took on soft low tones that for the moment settled the pony down.

Having registered Amy ran back dodging in and out amongst the crowd, number in hand, to the waiting pony and man. She wanted to hug Vic for being there, his stocky frame and bow legs were indeed a welcome sight.

"Here. Give it to me. C'mon, turn around." The short man took the number. The figure '5' was printed on a square piece of white fabric, with small safety pins at each corner. Vic turned her around and pinned the number on the back of her shirt.

"They asked me to watch for you. Bloody late y'are girl. There's four other entries in the Ladies Mile. Bloody great thoroughbreds they are. So this is Friska eh. Well he looks like he has some Arab in him. That's a good thing. Y' know Amy, this horse may be small, but I think he's everything you said he was." He talked on, calming her nerves with his voice.

Once the number was attached to the back of her shirt Vic took her shoulders in his hands and turned Amy to face him. He bent forward and looked into her eyes.

"Now Amy, hear me well. We have drawn you number one lane. Now that means you are against the rails. Y' get out to th' start and line up there and now girl." He bent lower. "Whatever happens, no matter what t'other horses do, y' stay against th' rails. Y'hear me?" Amy nodded, she could not speak. He gave her a little shake and said again, "No matter what, don't leave th' rails. Run all th'way beside th'rails. Y'got that?" Amy nodded again. "Okay. Then good luck to yer." He legged her up onto Friska with an expert lift. The pony immediately danced sideways, tossing his head and giving small bucks, Amy's body, tuned to his every move, went with him. Vic grinned,

"Get out there then."

Again Amy wanted to hug him, but with her hands full of hundreds of pounds of fighting horse she raised an eyebrow at Vic, grinned her 'thank-you' and turned Friska towards the four horses parading around the birdcage. She was the last lady rider to arrive in the birdcage, grateful to be kept from too many probing, curious eyes and hoping no one would notice her, she kept her eyes determinately ahead.

As Vic had said, the horses were big. A tall grey, carrying an older, tough-looking woman, wearing a smart, black riding habit, led the others around the dusty, circular path inside the birdcage. A white square of fabric carrying the number four was pinned to the back of her black jacket. Number three followed her, a light roan mare, easy to see from a long distance, skipped daintily, its young rider, skilfully holding the reins, controlled the excited horse. Halfway back in distance in the circle came a beautiful, high withered, black thoroughbred gleaming with health and strength. A strong, larger woman, rode proudly, as the tall, handsome horse strode calmly around the circle. She carried the number two, and the number one horse, also jet black, followed, dancing and working the bit against the reins, his rider looked not much older than Amy, and also, like Amy, wore only a white shirt with jodhpurs and riding boots.

Resplendent in his long, red riding coat, the clerk of the course, mounted on a big, beautiful grey horse, blew three blasts on his brass horn to call the five lady riders from the birdcage and onto the track. The tough, older woman and her big grey, led them all out, as each horse following several seconds behind the other, allowed them time for a warm-up canter, down the course and towards the starting line.

'One day, we will have flash starting gates, like the ones in England,' Amy had heard Vic say, what a thing to remember Amy muttered to herself as she held Friska back, the butterflies in her stomach had again begun to rise as tightness clamped into her throat. Amy concentrated on Friska holding him steady as they cantered after the others, he bent his head in a beautiful arch, bounding with energy and eager to run, working his mouth against her as she controlled him keeping him separate from the other horses, her number five out of sequence as she brought him dancing sideways in excitement up to the start line.

"Ladies!" The start steward strode up and down on the track before them, completely unconcerned that any horse might break away and run him down, he called them into line. The horses, sweating and excited, milled around in agitation.

"The numbers are out of kilt." He yelled so they would not miss his words. "We got number five, that's you." He pointed at Amy. "Against the rails, and number four." He nodded at the jet black with its young rider. "You miss, are on the outside. Right now, I want y'all t' calm those mounts of yours as much as they'll let you, I got "are y'ready" and when I drop th' flag y' just go. Y'all got that? Everyone clear?"

CHAPTER 13

THE OLD KUIA, sucked on her now empty pipe, and waited. She quietly sang the songs of her ancestors. Songs of the spirits her tohunga line had passed down in secrecy to her. She would soon pass them on to her Mokopuna Joe. He would be ready in another year. Joe was destined to enter the pakeha church, although he did not yet know it. It was written in him. She could see a strong bright light that surrounded Joe and many of his friends, a light that shone from within. It was the same with both Maori and Pakeha. Not for all Maori though, plenty of darkness in Maori, too much darkness, but the light would come in when they were ready, for it too was written. Only the light would flood out the darkness in the people. Huia reached into her deep pocket, bringing out an old fob watch, she glanced at the time, then she once again took up the carved walking stick and ran her fingers over the intricately carved patterns.

The carvings were for her tupuna and they told the story of her ancestry. A beautifully carved taniwha curled its way down from the top of the stick, entwining the patterns, weaving them together, its head forming the knob that fitted perfectly into Huia's palm. She rubbed the warm familiar lines, her hand following the taniwha, as it curved its way down the carved stick, bringing together the ancestor stories in beautiful harmony.

Once again she held the knob, the head of the taniwha, to her forehead, transferring the life force from herself into the stick, then she returned to the bush and the group of stones. Chanting a sweet karakia, she called the waiting spirits; spirits of speed and strength. She stood, facing north towards the race track, standing on the koru that she had earlier placed on the centre stone and began her melodic chant.

*   *   *

"READY!" A second later the Steward dropped his flag. "Go!"

Five horses leapt away and raced down the track.

Amy and Friska were quickly left behind as the larger horses, fresh and ready to run, bounded away.

In the large, open grandstand Doug and Katie Brookfield had excellent seats. He had just returned with two cups of tea for them when the Ladies Mile Steeplechase started. Doug had not looked at the line up of names for the race, but Katie had. She had turned quite pale and her heart had done a complete somersault when she saw Amy's name on the programme. Then she understood, ah yes... suddenly the long runs after school with the pony, the feeling that Amy was carrying a secret that she could not share, it all became very clear. Although Katie's heart had flipped over when she read the riders' names a warm surge followed as she recognised her daughter's self-knowledge. Katie's hand trembled as she took the cup of tea from her husband's hand, she gave a small nod towards the race names as she handed him the programme. Unthinking, he responded to their silent, familiar communication and looked at the names.

Doug dropped his cup of tea. Both cup and saucer broke as they hit the floor.

"Oh my GOD… Oh dear Lord… oh… " He looked disbelieving at Katie. He looked again at the programme, numbly he then looked out at the track and the horses in the Ladies Mile Steeplechase.

Friska and Amy were three lengths behind the bunch of racing horses. They were unmistakable. None of the riders wore hats, only the jockeys wore caps. Amy's brown golden hair flew out from under her hairband as Friska's flying main hid her face from view.

*   *   *

Huia the kuia, lifted her chant, holding her stick towards the north and the race track she called the spirits of speed and strength to come to Amy. She called them. Amy had stuck up for her mokupuna Joe. Her daughter's child. No Pakeha, in her life, had ever done that, stood up for a Maori and protected him like that. She called them forth. Go with her she called. Put wings on the pony's hooves. Take her beyond the other horses she called, pointing the taniwha's head towards the north. The stick began to tremble in her hands. The old woman held it strongly, continuing her call.

* * *

Doug Brookfield looked at his wife. "How could she...?" he croaked.

"Watch her Doug," Katie soothed. "Watch her and learn about your daughter. Be here now, with her."

"You knew?" He asked, feeling twice betrayed. "All this time you knew?"

"No Doug. You know better than that, but I did feel that she was up to something. Oh Doug. Look!"

The horses were still in a bunch, jumps were made as each one came up they seemed to fly the fences as if one entity. Amy and Friska were still behind as they came to the long hill that made the race famous. Up they went, the fences and the hill began to bring a separation to the small, galloping group.

Amy bent down low. She did not ride high as the others did. Once again she heard Huia saying 'y'ride like y' ride... be you.' She felt Friska double his strength as they came to the long hill. He seemed to take off and fly, as the big horses began to flag in their speed, Friska increased his. They flew by inside the other horses, over the next fence and on up the rise, they ran on with only the big grey ahead of them, and he ran against the rails, his big hooves threw up large clods of turf that hit Amy in the face, his grey tail streamed out behind him. Lying along Friska's neck, Amy urged him on, but the big grey blocked their way against the rails, only the outside of the track was clear, and she could get through if she eased Friska over to pass on the outside, there was plenty of room, but then, she heard Vic's words, 'No matter what happens… stay on the rail.'

*   *   *

The old kuia lifted her voice higher, her chants coming harder and pointing the stick towards the race track it shook more urgently, as if it had a life of its own. SPEED AND STRENGTH …she called…… bring to them both GREAT SPEED AND STRENGTH.

*   *   *

Doug and Katie gripped each others hands in unconscious tightness. "Ride him Amy," her father whispered. "Ride him…"

The big grey leapt the fence at the top of the hill, unknowingly moving out several feet as he did so, Friska shot through the gap that opened up between the big horse and the rails, Amy went with him, part of him, as if they were one creature, it was so fast, the big grey was suddenly two lengths behind, as his rider, startled at the unexpected speed of the smaller horse, had to check her mount for the next fence. Over the top of the hill they went and down the other side, flying over the low brush fence downhill, and onto the flat, two hundred yards of clear race track, that had opened up before them, in the run down the home stretch and to the winning post. Friska hardly touched the earth in an almost unreal pace, pulling ahead of the other four and into the straight, as gathering strength with the long hill behind them the other horses began to gain on him, their longer strides making up the distance that separated them from the speeding pony, in the stands the crowd roared, rising to their feet in one movement as the small horse held the lead. Could he stay there? The big horses gained steadily, but the speeding pony flew, his young rider buried in his main, flying with him, as they raced past the finishing post, Friska's nose in front, just barely, but nevertheless, he was in the front.

The crowd went wild.

The cheers thundered out for the small pony that came in ahead of the big ones.

Katie's eyes sparkled as her tears ran unhindered down her cheeks, her husband stood exhausted, silenced and bursting with pride for the daughter he had seen fly by to victory.

*   *   *

The kuia laid down her stick. She knelt on the hard stone in the centre of the circle and gave a long and quiet thank you to the spirits that had come when she called.

"It be good justice," she told them. "It be right. I thank you…"

CHAPTER 14

AMY'S HEART RACED with joy. She wanted to jump off the pony and turn cartwheels down the centre of the race track. Hundreds of cartwheels. She wanted to stand up on Friska's back and touch the sky, while he danced beneath her. We did it. We did it. We did it. She lightened her grip on Friska's reins as she steadied him down to a canter, and he, excited by the noise and the crowd, began to lift his feet in a prancing dance, as if he knew just what he had done. The clerk of the course trotted up to them, clipping a lead rein onto Friska's bridle, he smiled at Amy, and led both, girl and pony, back down the track to the birdcage.

People and horses were everywhere. Many of the spectators in the grandstand had come down to crowd around at the rails that surrounded the space they called the birdcage. Amy and Friska were led into the centre where a small platform was covered in bright cloth and where several people stood waiting for her. Vic suddenly appeared, a huge grin practically splitting his face into two. He helped Amy to dismount, unsaddled Friska and he led them along the shell path to the large scales for the weigh-in.

"Well done Amy. Champion.....Just champion. Y' ll have th' speeches first, then y'cn weigh in." he chuckled.

"W-what speeches? What for?"

"You'll see." He chuckled some more.

Suddenly, no longer excited, Amy felt afraid. She glanced around at the milling, noisy crowd and it was then that she saw her father and mother.

They were standing, almost lost, amongst the dense crowd. With a small cry at what she had done, Amy forgot where she was and ran across the small space to where they stood.

"Oh Mum, Dad… Oh I am sorry… I really did not mean, I mean I did, but then I didn't. It was just that… It just seemed to be… a…"

"Hush Amy. Hush. It's all right now. We'll talk of it later." Her father reached over the rails and gave her a hug.

Amy wanted to burst into tears.

Her mother ducked under the rail and held her close. She did not speak.

"Come on Amy." Vic was still there, sheltering and shepherding her and leading Friska. "Bring them with you. You've gotta have th' speeches."

Her father also climbed under the rail and Amy walked between them, holding their hands, back to the platform. The Mayor of Auckland, dressed in robes and chain, was waiting with the race officials. Speeches were made, congratulating her, a large wreath of flowers was hung over Friska's neck, as he stood quietly at last. He tossed his head in acknowledgement making it difficult for the Mayor as he attached a purple ribbon rosette to his bridle. To Amy, it all seemed completely unreal.

* * *

Mokupuna Joe stood back from the crowd. He watched from an empty horse stall, just high enough to see all that was going on. Joe did not want to approach Amy there was just too much hu ha going on. His fingers rubbed the pound notes, new and crisp, in his pocket. Joe had saved up a whole two pounds from selling smoked eel to the Ellerslie butcher. He had known that the kuia was helping Amy, and he came to the race track to put his hard earned money on Friska to win.

Joe knew exactly what the money in his pocket was for.

* * *

The ride home was so very different from the one that they had made that morning. Gone was the dancing and prancing as Friska walked quietly along the dry road, his head loose from any restriction of the reins. Amy sat back in the saddle, as the pony reached out occasionally and grabbed at the juicy grass alongside the road. He ambled, relaxed and loose, back the way they had come only that morning.

Amy felt so badly she almost felt ill. The elation and excitement of her win was long gone, replaced by an agony of despair. She could see the pain in her father's eyes. Oh, he had hugged her; he had put aside his true reactions to be there for her in those moments that followed the race, but it had been there in his eyes. It was unmistakable. He looked so confused and hurt. All her life he had been there for her, loving her, helping her with her homework, building boats with her to float on the creek. Boats made from scraps of wood that often sank, the water bubbling up through the boards it made both of them laugh and they would start again. Amy remembered the day her father brought Friska home. He had ridden the pony home the four miles from the Westfield sale yards where he had purchased the pony from a farmer from the Waikato. It had been a special day. The pony was a gift for her tenth birthday and Amy and her mother had seen him riding down the road in the late afternoon. She vividly remembered running to meet him and clapping her hands with joy as her father had climbed down and swung her up into the saddle. He led both pony and girl the remaining few hundred yards of the way home. As Amy dismounted, she had hugged Friskas' neck and she had known from that moment that they would be life long friends.

Friska lifted his head, pricking his ears forward and quickening his pace, as they neared his home paddock, it had been a long time since his last feed. Amy dismounted and led him through the gate into the yard. She watered and fed him, crooning to him as she brushed away the sweat of the day. Once done, the thoughts came flooding back. Knowing her parents would soon return, Amy sat in the hay and sobbed.

CHAPTER 15

Doug and Katie walked slowly home. In his right hand he carried the large silver cup that Amy had won, his other hand held one of Katie's. Doug still did not know what to think. He shook his head in disbelief. His daughter had misled him. How could she have done that? Could he ever trust her again? Doug did not know how he felt or what to think of it all. A part of him was proud of her, elated at watching girl and pony ride such an exhilarating race. Yet a part of him felt very betrayed. The daughter he loved so dearly had clearly lied to him, had deliberately misled him, he did not want to believe it, but he had to believe it.

Katie was silent beside him aware of his inner struggle. She said nothing, allowing his private thoughts to tumble over and over. Katie knew that, somehow, he and Amy would work through this. Feeling his confusion, she squeezed his hand, her own excitement had not diminished. Watching Amy and Friska fly past the winning post ahead of the other horses had been a thrill she would remember forever. She glanced at her husband just as he, at the same time, glanced at her, he shook his head again in a small movement and looked away. Lines of pain settled on his face. Together, quietly, each with their own thoughts, they walked the two miles home.

"I'll put the kettle on," said Katie as they walked up the front steps. "We both need a cup of tea." She knew this sounded hollow and foolish, but it broke the spell of silence that had held them for so long. Doug followed her inside.

They were halfway through their tea when Amy came in from the paddock. Her eyes were red and swollen from crying. She stood in the doorway and looked across at her much loved father as he sat sipping his tea, he returned her look. Then, with a small cry, Amy ran across the room and knelt down at his feet, wrapping her arms over his knees. Her tears began all over again.

Doug stroked her hair, this daughter who was so much of his life. After several minutes, he reached down and lifted her up onto his knee. Amy had not sat on her father's knee since she was a small child, now she was big and awkward. She sat on his knee and hid her head in the curve of his neck, as he rocked her, very gently, soothing her sobs.

"Oh daddy, I'm so so so sorry. I'd... d... didn't mean to hurt you, b... b... but you n... never really said no, not really, you said..., but not ever, actually said no, and my m... mind just was so str... strong in knowing we could w... win the race ...I j j just..." Her whole body heaving with big sobs.

"Shush. Shush now Amy. It's all right."

"B... But no, it's not all right. It was s... so so wrong of me. I was so very very sure. We trained so hard, and Friska was so right to run in th... the race. It was so hard not t... t... to say anything, but I just knew s s... so knew th... that you wouldn't understand," and she began to sob uncontrollably again.

Doug rocked his daughter gently. He looked across at Katie. He had not listened to Amy. He knew that now. He had not allowed her tell him how she felt, or how much it meant to her to ride the pony in the race, and he had not been able to see her ability nor see the confidence she had gained in herself.

He had not seen her self-knowledge.

A long sigh escaped him. The sigh relaxed his whole body as he began to recognise all that had taken place, all that had led them to his moment. Doug sighed again.

"Amy," he said quietly. "I too need to be sorry. Ssh m'darlin, no more crying. I did not listen to you. Did not see the truth, and y'know m'darling, y' always need to live in the truth."

"B b… but Daddy, I didn't lie to you, I just d d… didn't tell you the truth."

"Shush. I see that now. That's not what I meant. I mean, well, you've been a child all of these years. I still want you to be a child, but you are not. You are halfway to being a grown woman and yet are still half a child. And Amy, you saw your own strength. You saw your own ability. Of all the things a parent would want for their child, to see them in their own strength is the greatest, because, my beautiful daughter, and I know, really, this is something that people never say to each other, but it is your own, very personal God knowledge. Something inside that gives you a self-knowing, that no other person can know, or understand. I should have seen that and I should have listened to you. It is I Amy, who am sorry."

Katie looked across the table at them both. She relaxed and sipped her tea, and the small smile, missing from her face for many hours, slipped back in.

"Now Amy." Doug moved her onto a chair, as her mother poured her a cup of tea. "The race Steward gave me this for you." He took a narrow envelope from the inside pocket of his suit and laid it on the table before her.

"What is it?"

"Well. Open it and see."

Curiously, Amy tore open the top of the envelope. From the inside she drew out ten one pound notes and one ten shilling note. Completely surprised, she looked at her father.

"It's the prize money. You won it."

TEN GUINEAS!" cried Amy. "IT'S A FORTUNE.

CHAPTER 16

M OKUPUNA JOE HAD made his decision. He sat in the early morning on the log outside his kuia's shack and, not for the first time, counted the notes from his jacket pocket. Joe had it all planned. Had even had it planned before going to the races last Saturday. His two pounds had become sixty, and all because Amy and her pony had won the Ladies Mile Steeplechase. Joe counted the notes carefully, five ten pound notes and two five pound notes, he then rolled the five tens and one of the five pound notes together and secured the roll with a rubber band before putting them back in the hidden pocket inside his jacket.. He kept the remaining five pound note loose, fingering it thoughtfully for a moment, he then pocketed it safely along side the others and set off at a fast walk through the bush.

The village was quiet this morning with few people around. Rays of light from the warm sun made patterns like some crazy quilt as they fell onto the pavement through the gaps in the low buildings.

Joe usually kept away from the village but today was different. There would be no school for him today. Today would be the next step in his long term plan but first he would buy his kuia a gift. He walked boldly into the menswear shop, suddenly startled by the bell, set off by the opening of the door that jangled beside his head.

Reggie Kennett was leaning on the counter reading the morning newspaper. A shaft of sunlight lit the counter creating a warm area that Reggie was making full use of. He had received one other customer that morning when Amy had visited him. She brought him the ten shillings agreed to in the deal they had made and she had received back the three pieces she had tried so hard to sell. Her visit had brightened his morning even more than the sunlight but he had not told her that he had placed ten shillings on Friska to win the Ladies Mile Steeplechase. He had won fifteen pounds when he backed Friska at the races.

Hearing the doorbell Reggie looked up, taking in the Maori boy at a glance.

"Good morning my lad." His jovial voice instantly made Joe relax and eased the nervousness that he felt on entering the shop. Joe usually avoided Pakeha men. He did not feel comfortable with them, feeling that they looked down on him in some way and inside himself he had refused to allow their attitude to take any hold. Every human being has a right to his place on this earth, he would tell himself, and no man is either more or less than another.

"And how" continued Reggie "can we help you on this fine morning?"

"Um, well, if it's okay, I would like to buy my kuia a new pipe."

"Would you now." Reggie studied his new visitor taking in the slight nervousness and the fresh country look that accompanied Joe. "And could it be that your kuia is old Huia? Who lives over the hill in the bush?"

Joe became suddenly wary. He had known for some time that the village people mocked the old lady. Often it had puzzled him, for in his home village there were many old women who still wore the moko. The purple tattoo tapped into their chins. In their young days the moko, given to only a very few was a mark of great respect among the young Maori people, yet here in Ellerslie, so near to the city of Auckland, the local citizens made the old kuia and her moko an object of ridicule. It troubled Joe greatly, it was, he thought, unfair and unkind.

"Why do you ask?" Joe faced him bravely.

"Ah my boy. I know some people do not really understand your kuia and her moko. Please don't put me in there with them. Y'see I grew up in Morrinsville. We had many of the old ones then still wearing the moko. We had th' men too. Heavily tattooed they still were back then, many of your Maori people were still living in their pas. The local Chief in our area had total control over his people."

"Did he?" Joe forgot his suspicions and became suddenly curious. "What was that like? Do you remember what he wore?"

"Of course! It's as easy as if it were yesterday, he was pretty old, and, well, I was only a child let's see, that would be in about, um, nineteen hundred and five? Yep, about then I would reckon. There were many old tattooed Maori, back then and really most of them wore European clothes, I don't remember seeing any of them in your native dress, Nah, I never saw anyone wearing the native dress, I s'pose that the European style of clothes were warmer and easier to wear."

"Gee. Maori people in pas. I would love to have lived back then."

"No y' wouldn't." Reggie interrupted Joe's train of thought. "Nah… all that fighting and eating each other, taking each other as slaves. Nah m'boy. It's good that we can't go back."

"My kuia says that we went into darkness after we signed some Treaty, or something, with the Government."

"Into the darkness eh…" Reggie rubbed his chin. "Well I dunno 'bout that, I reckon your Chiefs were a pretty smart bunch."

"Smart?" Joe almost jerked back in surprise. "That's not what I have been told. I thought they were dumb. Y'know, a bit like children. Led down th' garden path by the Government, they were."

"What's y' name son?" Reggie leaned over his counter, studying this interesting young Maori boy, it was very rare for a Maori to enter his shop and this boy was most unusual.

"I am Joe Manukau, I am from Pokeno." Joe decided not to call him "Sir" he was sick of the word "Sir". At school all of the male teachers were called "Sir".

"Reggie Kennett, at your service, and pleased I am to meet you Joe Manukau," at that, the shop man reached over the counter, took Joe's hand and gave it a friendly shake. Completely taken by surprise for no-one had ever shaken his hand before, Joe, suddenly proud, returned the hand shake firmly.

"Joe Manukau. That's a fine name. Well Joe, maybe you should listen to your kuia. Trouble with th' young ones is, they never listen to th' kuias, 'n don't you ever let anyone tell you that those early Chiefs didn't know what they were doing. Smart buggers those. You know, we would all be speaking French if those early Chiefs had not signed that treaty."

Joe was completely stunned. He had never heard such words. Most of his understanding had come from hearing the talk on the Marae. They were always going on about being 'done' by the Government. They met on the Marae whenever there was something to celebrate or if someone important had died, then all of his people came from the outlying areas to honour the event. Joe's mouth fell open at what Reggie had just said.

"Speaking French? I'm sorry, I don't understand. Why do you say we would all be speaking French?"

"Y' know young Joe." Reggie warmed to his subject, "Great strength comes from knowing th' past. If y' know the past then y' can, much better understand, th' present. I went to th' Great War y' know and fought alongside young Maori men just like you. Those men were th' best soldiers a man could have beside him. Still of the warrior race they were, the most noble and brave men I have ever met. Y'know Joe," he leaned across the counter as his voice dropped. "Those Maori soldiers, some of them straight from the bush laid down their lives for their mates. They would go into places where no one else would go. They had a sixth sense that gave them an ability to anticipate the enemy in a way I have never seen. They would sort of, um.... well they would sit together around one fella in a circle looking out, and this fella he would sort of sit in the middle of their circle with his eyes closed and they would stay like that for hours, then, the one in the centre would begin to chant and mumble. Y' had to be there to understand, but those Maori soldiers would listen to the central one as they would a tohunga, and he would tell them what was coming and how to combat it. Talked to the spirits they did. And my best mate Tane, he would share it with me as much as he could. Honour they had. There were no lies or deceit in any of those Maori soldiers. Tane said the spirits would never come to their assistance if there were any lies or deceit in them."

"If y'know and understand th'past, it makes you strong." Reggie continued. "Now that there Treaty, that came from Ngapuhi."

"Ngapuhi?" Joe spat out the name. "Those murderers!"

"Now Joe they were not all murderers. Yeh," he held up his hand, stopping Joe's next words. "Yep I know th' story. Got to know when I fought with all those fellas in France. Th' Ngapuhi came down th' coast and killed off all th' southern tribes with their muskets, well wasn't really a fight they said, seeing th' tribes down here had never seen a musket."

Joe glared at the shopman. How could he stand there and talk like this. No one, no pakeha anyway, had the right to talk like this. His anger began to rise inside him in a wave of fury, as his fists curled themselves into a ball, wanting to strike the man. How dare he say such false words!

Reggie saw and understood his reaction. Years of living and working with his Maori mates, had given him much insight into their ways. He spoke their language fluently. He spoke it now, softly, with the hum that the language inspired, speaking to the heart of the young warrior before him.

The shop owner told Joe in the soft tongue of his own Maori people, how the French had come to their land many years ago, in a time when only the Maori lived here. Of how, unknowingly the visitors had broken the sacred tapu of the land, and had stamped on the Ngapuhi pride. As Joe listened to the soft words, he could see the pictures in his mind. He saw the French Captain abuse the Ngapuhi and he saw the Ngapuhi Chief and his warriors, who killed and ate the visitors. UTU, he thought, the law of the land. The French, who survived, climbed into their great sail boats and they blasted the nearby Maori village with their canons before sailing away from the land. The Ngapuhi would never forget. The village and everyone in it had been destroyed. Joe had heard about that in the songs on the Marae where the women sang the stories of the past weaving them in unforgettable legend into the songs of today.

"Your kuia," Reggie continued, still in the soft language of the Maori people. "She knows and understands all of this. She says that the Maori people are in the darkness did that mean that they were in the light?" Joe nodded, spellbound. "Aye." said Reggie, "In the light, why? Because the people of light came and helped the Maori to change. To see a new way. A way of no more fighting with each other, a way of peaceful co-existence, and when later,on, more Frenchmen came to take the country, to make it a French colony, the Ngapuhi Chiefs went to the people of light and asked them to make this place an English colony."

Mokupuna Joe and Reggie sat together for a long time. In the dialect of Joe's people, Reggie told him many things. He reminded him also of the honour and pride of his people, of the knowledge of his kuia, that this knowledge would be passed on to the next generation and that this is a precious gift.

At the end of their talk, Reggie reached for a beautiful, shiny, new pipe, and two tins of "Old Gold" tobacco. He would not let Joe pay for it.

"It's for all those men who fought with me," he said, with reverence as he put the items in a paper bag. They parted, pressing their noses together in the Maori way, a hongi, an exchange of life force between two people.

CHAPTER 17

I T WAS NEARING noon when Joe Sigley saw the young Maori boy swinging towards him down the road. They grow 'em big, he thought, as Mokupuna Joe, tall and athletic, drew closer. The young Maori, often a visitor to their farm, was always welcome. He and Tom had been friends since they were small children.

The farmer pulled his boots off and sat down on the step to wait for him.

"G'day young Joe, what brings you here in the late morning. Tom is at school, thought you would be to, here, come and have a seat." He moved over making room on the wide step.

"Well, I would have been here earlier, at least that was the plan." Joe sat down on the shared space. "But on my way, I got rather delayed."

They sat together for several minutes, without speaking. Young Joe trusted his friend's father. He had often visited Tom's home and been treated as a valued human being by old Joe. That was why he had come. On leaving Reggie's shop, he spent much of the morning sitting in the nearby bush, going over what had been said. The conversation had shaken him deeply. Now he was here he could not go home or to school before completing his mission. He was grateful that the older man did not pry into the cause of the delay.

"You know," the farmer began. "It is strange calling you Joe and me Joe. Seems a bit ridiculous, so I have decided to call you Joseph. It's a noble and fine name, is Joseph."

For the second time that morning, Mokupuna Joe was taken

completely by surprise by an older pakeha. A warm flow of energy ran through him, and seemed to fill his whole body with its glow. Joseph? He liked it. He liked it very much.

The five pound note he had kept back to buy his kuia's pipe and tobacco had been returned to the roll of notes held by the rubber band in his pocket. He stroked them with his fingers as he looked for the words he needed. 'When y' stuck, just say th' simple truth', he could hear his kuia say.

"If you do not mind," he started, haltingly. "I really need some help."

"You only have to say young Joseph," the older man said kindly. "I will help in any way I can. You look as if y' have th' world on your shoulders. Is that kuia of yours in good health? Must be pretty old by now. It must be a great comfort to her, having you live with her."

"Thank you, but she's fine, tough as old boots she is." He took the notes from his pocket and unrolling them from the rubber band he laid them, all sixty pounds, carefully on the ground at their feet.

"Hm…," older Joe said after a long pause. "That, my boy, is quite a tidy sum of money."

Once more the trust was there he could feel it, he knew then that he was making the right decision. That his friend's father was the person he should come to.

"I won it on Saturday at the Ellerslie races. I backed Amy to win on her pony and she did. She was, they said, a rank outsider, and I placed a bet on. I placed a whole two pounds to win on Amy. My kuia told me how to do it."

Old Joe burst out laughing. He laughed and laughed and laughed. Newly-named Joseph began to grin, then catching the humour of it, he joined in.

"That, is one of th' best bits of news I have had in a long time," chuckled old Joe. "Ho Ho, heh, heh. Oh the way our lives twist and turn. I'm sorry son, didn't mean to laugh at you, just at the beauty of th' whole damn thing. Heh heh heh, sixty quid. S'a great deal of money." Then, wiping his eyes on his rough sleeve, he added, "I heard about Amy's race. I reckon that we will be hearing about it for a long time. Sort of thing that becomes a bit of a legend eh, spunky girl that Amy, rides like a dream she does. Heh heh thirty to one.....” He chuckled again. “Y'know Joseph, it makes a man realise, that the next generation, will take us forward to even greater and better things. Hope I'm around to watch it all.”

“Oh but you are. I mean you will be.” Joseph could not think of the older man not being here.

“Well... I'm here for some time to come. So tell me, how can I help?”

“I want to buy a house for my family.”

“Your family?” It was the older mans turn to be taken by surprise. “Where are your family?”

“They live in the bush at the back of Pokeno. They live in a raupo whare. There are ten of us.”

“Oh my good Lord,” old Joe muttered quietly. So many Maori lived in this way but it was not the same as their old way in the past. Changes had come, some good, some bad. New diseases, land loss and liquor helped to bring bad times and too many early deaths to the Maori people.

“I was sent as mokupuna to my kuia,” Joseph looked down at his hands. The notes sat on the ground at their feet, he reached out and gathered a small stone and placed it on top of them, ensuring that no sudden breeze would lift them away. “I love my kuia but I miss my family very much. Sometimes I go and visit them but it is never for long because I was given to my kuia to be her companion and help.”

“Aye. It's th' way of your people lad and a good way it is.”

“I looked at all of the house prices in the newspaper. I have been watching for a very long time and, oh ….I have been walking past that house just out past the school, the one the vicar used to live in, y' know, that old white one with the big gum tree behind it, it has been empty since they built the new one by the church and moved them all in, the vicar and his family I mean.”

“You are a very smart young man. So you have been wanting this for a long time. Your plan is very good very good indeed, but what about your kuia? Will you all live there? Ten of you and two more?”

“Oh no Mr. Sigley. Oh no. My kuia would never move. I can't

explain it, but she would never move, would never live in a pakeha house."

"No need to try and explain son, no need at all, but your father and your mother, how would they get on, coming here from the bush?"

"My Dad, he works in the Huntly coal mine. He goes down by train every Monday and then comes home on Friday. It is too hard for my Mum, her fingers look swollen and sore. My sister, she is Hana, she looks after them all," he said proudly. "Hana is beautiful, she is strong and proud. My Dad could get a job on the Onehunga wharves, there are notices up in the village looking for men for loading the boats. Oh it would get him out of those coal mines," he raced on, warming to his plans, excited to be talking of the family he so seldom saw. "Th' kids could come to school. Too many Maori can't read or write, most of them live too far out, still in the whares most of the people. It's no good. It's no good at all!"

Old Joe reached over and put his arm around young Joseph's shoulder.

"And would you like me to find out for you how much the house would cost? Shall I talk to the pakeha people for you?"

Joseph picked up the sixty pounds of notes and held them out towards his friend's father.

"No. I would like, if you don't mind, to ask you to buy the house for me and my family."

CHAPTER 18

THE WARM SUN shone on through the trees, as Amy and Friska glided amongst them. They were on the top of the hills above the Ellerslie village and Friska, sensing that a long run was about to happen, began his endless dance, as the plains running towards Mt Wellington came into sight.

A wide vista opened up before them, leading Amy's eyes across the plains to the volcanic cone that rose over two hundred feet, from between where she and the pony stood and to the wide Tamaki river beyond. Friska's dance increased, as Amy guided him down the slope towards the plain. He swung sideways, then back across the path, as she kept him steady.

"Take it easy," she whispered to him. "Just get us down this slope through the trees and then you can have your way. C'mon boy. Easy… Easy." But he knew her too well, and expecting any minute to be allowed to run, he kept tossing his head impatiently.

Amy let him go at the bottom of the hill. The pony, familiar with the track, soon reached a breakneck speed as he galloped across the miles of flat plain towards the beckoning volcanic cone. They flew, girl and pony, leaping the patches of scrub and ditches as they came up, dodging the trees that stood in clumps along the way as they neared the base of the mountain. Instinctively Friska slowed, tossing his head, coming to a trot and following the track, as it led them amongst the dense bush at the end of the plain and onto the narrow path that led up the side of the mountain. Amy held him to a fast walk, easing him, keeping him from racing up the mountain side as he wanted to do, conserving his strength to keep him from blowing himself out.

The path had been formed by sheep and was seldom used. It clung half hidden to the mountain, spiralling in a wide circle around the steep sides and up towards the summit. It required care and concentration to keep from falling over the edge as together girl and pony climbed the path to the top.

Upon reaching the summit Amy pulled up and jumped off Friska. She loosened the girth on the saddle allowing him to re-load his lungs with deep, great breaths she then led him quietly to a lone cabbage tree. Still fighting fit from his race training he quickly recovered from the steep climb. Amy tied him to the tree and set off on foot to explore. She had ridden here many times before and never ceased to enjoy the wide views of the countryside that flowed away to the south of the river. A wide rim of almost flat terrain formed Mt Wellington summit. The deep volcanic crater fell steeply away inside the rim making it seem like a giant basin, or some oversized mixing bowl. Grass and trees grew densely within the long extinct crater. Deep trenches, some two hundred yards apart, cut through the rim, where, in earlier times, the local Maori tribe had built their defensive pa. A legacy of the past that still today had European settlers marvelling at the engineering skill of these early people.

Looking back the way she had come, Amy could see across the plains to the Ellerslie village in the distance and then beyond the village over low-lying hills to the sky line, where the sharp outline of the hill with one tree on the summit dominated the surrounding area. She could just see a long line of horse drawn vehicles coming around the base of the hills, following the road that she and Friska had just travelled.

It was Saturday, the day of the annual district picnic. Everyone was invited, from the village and from the surrounding area, and each year they came, old and young, harnessing their horses to whatever farm vehicle they might have. Most still used horse-drawn transport but this year some of the villagers and farmers drove automobiles.

Each year the local settlers would set off for the spit in the Tamaki River, a distance of some five miles from Ellerslie. The spit was a favourite gathering place and the late autumn days still held much warmth, a time when the heavy farm work of the summer had ceased. It would take the next hour for them to reach their destination.

Amy did not want to travel with the slow train. Some of her friends would be down there on their horses, riding alongside the family carts, and later, she would ride home with them but for now she wanted to run. To ride alone and fast. To feel free.

Amy ran around the rim of the crater. On the eastern side, near where Friska was tethered, she looked out towards the spit. It was easy to see. A long stretch of sand that pointed, like an extended slender finger, into the wide river. The river sparkled like a magic fairytale ribbon in the early morning light. It flowed from the low hills in the west winding its way across the distant farmland dipping its way out of sight, only to appear again, here and there between the low hills, in a taunting, teasing glitter on its way to the sea that lay to the east. From where she stood, the lowland sloped away across a wide area to the river. The small village of Panmure peeped out of its cradle, where the new bridge cut the river in two halves. On the south side of the river, wide, green hills rolled together, mixed with stands of the native forest, as if sewn by some master embroiderer, into an intricate pattern. She could see south for miles. She stretched her arms out wide, as if trying to embrace it all.

One by one the slow moving wagon train carrying the picnickers arrived at the spit. Dust from the road trailed behind them as they rumbled onto the wide grassy space that bordered the river. Happy to have arrived, the children mounted on ponies, raced ahead while their seated mothers called out to take care. Amy joined them as Friska pranced and danced looking excited by the other horses and putting out a challenge to them to race. Some ninety farm carts and drays drove in. Some had smart gigs others slow cumbersome wagons.

Fathers and big brothers took charge of the unloading, it was a gala of laughter and pandemonium as trestle tables were unfolded and set up. Mothers sisters and Aunts, unloaded their abundant cooking, covering the tables with baskets of food, chickens, pies, cakes, milk, sugar and tea teamed together with the many water billies which were filled with water from the nearby stream and placed on swiftly made fires.

"Look out! Hah. Stupid nag tried to kick me."

"Go on…. Get this rope run out, we can tie all of the horses in two lines. Look at those new motor cars, dunno if I would want one of those."

"Bet y'would if someone gave you one. Can't we get all these wagons and carts parked at the end of the field? Leave plenty of room for the cricket match."

"Look at those women would you. Did you ever see so much kissing and hugging?"

It was a day of fun, games, swimming and exploring. The womenfolk set out rugs and cushions at the eastern end of the beach in the shade of low hanging pohutukawa trees. The hillside at that end of the beach, gave shelter from the breezes that came in from the sea. The spit was abundant with cockles and tuatua, the low tide inviting the younger members to gather them.

Dressed in their swimming costumes Amy and Pammy set off with a bucket. They chose a spot farther out and with water around their knees they dug their hands into the muddy, sandy bottom and began to fill the bucket with juicy shellfish. Many other shellfish gatherers around them shouted and laughed as they jostled for the best places.

"There are so many cockles, those boys want to hog our spot… and oh look, darn them, they're starting a mud fight." Amy whispered to Pammy.

"Let's hope they keep it to themselves. Hey, are we in a good spot! Look there are hundreds here." Pammy scooped up further handfuls.

BLAP. A clod of mud hit Pammy in the back of her neck, the unexpected impact knocked her onto her hands and knees in the water.

"Who threw that?" she yelled climbing back up. "You miserable muck munchers!"

Four boys, led by Tom, came wading fast toward them. Pammy grabbed up large handfuls of mud.

"Hang onto our bucket Amy. The devils are after our cockles!" She threw the mud straight at the invaders. Amy grabbed the bucket and headed for the shore.

"Cut her off! Tim get her!" Tom wished his mate Joseph had come. He was faster than Tim.

Tim ran for Amy and made a grab for the loaded bucket. Amy swung it and caught him, with a full whack, in his stomach, winded, Tim toppled backwards into the water.

"Oooppss! Sorry!" She grinned at him as she ran for the shore, leaving him gasping for breath.

"Heh heh," chuckled Pammy, as she watched Amy race with their food hoard on to the firm sand, and head for the campfire the fathers, had built. "Serve you right! Go and get your own cockles you lazy, mud slinging monsters!"

"Get her!" leader Tom yelled. Handfuls of mud splattered Pammy from four angles. She answered by turning and wading further into the river, then she washed the mud off by diving beneath the surface and swimming out of range.

"Enough! We have enough food to feed an army," came the inevitable call from a watching father. "Come and make yourselves useful! We need plenty of firewood to cook these."

Endless piles of buttered bread were piled on plates over a large, white cloth. It quickly became another contest, taking the soft, home baked slices and covering them with the freshly cooked shellfish. People milled about in every direction, as children ran amongst them. A young mother grabbed her toddler as, fascinated with the colour, he reached out to the fire trying to grasp a red ember. The large fire had burned down, and the smouldering remains made a hot bed for cooking the vast quantities of gathered shellfish.

After lunch they played cricket. Amy did not like cricket. It was just too slow, but it was join in or be left out so she joined in. The smaller children ran around played tag, hide and seek and explored their new surroundings. Fathers stood in groups, shared their stories and caught up on the latest farming methods. They joined in the game or not as the mood took them.

Lazily the afternoon wore on. The clear, mellow day and warm sun, brought a relaxing atmosphere to them all. The breeze carried a strong smell of salt in from the nearby sea and as the tide rose a long net was taken out into the river and set to trap fish coming in to feed. Amy slipped off to check Friska. She had decided to take him to the nearby stream for a drink for the horses had been standing, strung out along the stretched rope, for several hours.

A leather halter with a long rope attached tethered Friska to the tall cabbage tree. There was plenty of shade, and Amy had placed both saddle and bridle against the tree trunk leaving him space to graze, separate from any biting or kicking farm horses. Amy untied the rope, wound it loosely in her hand and led him off towards the stream.

A sudden scream filled the air with an unearthly cry. Alarmed, Amy glanced at the river. Everyone seemed frozen in the moment, as a small five year-old boy, was swept away by the incoming tide the current, having built up just off the spit, carried him up river at a frightening pace. In an instant, the frozen spell was broken. People began to run, some into the river, others along the bank, but the current seemed to increase as the tiny head, now just a dot speeding with the water, turned round and around, disappeared and re-appeared, the one scream became more screams as panic set into the group.

Tom on his fast legs, sped from out of the cricket pitch. He raced along the shore, gradually gaining on the small, helpless, bobbing head. Only some four hundred yards of shoreline ran alongside the river before a steep bluff cut off the distant end of the beach where a small jetty had been built out into the river. Swiftly Tom left the others behind as he drew level with the small head and he dived into the water.

Amy did not stop to think. She swung onto Friska's back the pony sensing the frenzied moment, jumped immediately into a gallop out from under the trees, bareback and with only the halter, Amy and Friska charged towards the jetty at the end of the beach, Tom now had the boy, he could see what she was doing, he held his choking, terrified bundle above the fast moving water as pony and girl speeding along the shore, jumping bushes and rocks, raced to get ahead of them. Amy squeezed Friska with her legs, miraculously guiding him, they reached the jetty where, skidding to a stop, the movement carried her in one swift motion, forward over his shoulder her hand grabbing the halter where it sat between the pony's ears, taking it from his head in one continuous motion, her legs hit the ground at a full run, the heavy halter in her hand, the long rope in the other as she raced down the jetty swinging the halter around and around in a wide circle like a lasso, Tom trying to pull both himself and the struggling boy towards the jetty, read her every move as Amy swung the halter, it arched through the air hitting the water only a short distance ahead of the pair, Tom lunged, dragging the boy, reaching beneath the surface as the halter disappeared, his hand grasped it inches below .

Amy could not pull them in. She hung onto the rope, digging her bare feet into the jetty post. Racing in, the first father arrived, roughly pushing her aside as he grabbed the rope from her and began to pull both Tom and his sodden bundle slowly to the safety of the jetty.

Friska, startled and then alarmed at the crowd rushing towards him, and without Amy to guide him, spun around and bolted back the way they had come. Several people tried to stop him but he was not confident without his familiar rider communicating and joining in his every movement. Friska leapt away from them, spinning and jumping away over a large blackberry hedge.

No one could have seen it coming.

In fright and fear, Friska leaped the unknown hedge. On landing his near foreleg plunged straight into a deep hole hidden on the other side of the hedge, his speed sent him into a complete somersault in the air and he landed with a sickening thump on his back.

Amy had not seen him bolt. There was so much noise, so much was happening. Once she saw Tom and the limp, weeping boy, being lifted onto the jetty, she turned to look for Friska. He was nowhere to be seen. Alarmed and puzzled, she walked back down the jetty, scanning over the heads of the crowd, looking for his familiar shape. Friska was gone. A small group stood some distance away, and instinctively Amy headed towards them.

Friska was struggling to stand up. He was trying to walk, his forelegs gripping at the earth, his hind legs would not work, he snorted, his great eyes rolled in fear. Amy charged through the crowd pushing others aside.

"Friska!" she yelled "FRISKA !" the group of men close to the pony, their faces pale and set, looked at each other.

"His back is broken." Joe Sigley said quietly. "Does anybody have a gun?"

Each of them knew it was the only way. Men of the land, they faced the sadness of having to put an animal out of its misery and a broken back was impossible.

"I have a shotgun under my cart seat." It was said with great intake of breath. "Never know when you might find a rabbit for some tucker to take home."

"Get her out of here." Joe jerked his head toward Amy, his eyes full of anguish for her.

"FRISKA!" she yelled again. Pulling at the hands that held her. Hearing her the pony snorted in fear as he desperately bent the front of his body this way and that, in an effort to get up.

"NOOOOOO!"

It was Tom who grabbed her. Looking for her, walking from the jetty, he pushed through the crowd, reading at once the scene before him. Tom took Amy's arm wrapping it around his neck and half carried half dragged her away.

Amy could not walk. Her legs would not work. She tried to pull away from Tom. Reaching back towards Friska, she tried to speak, tried to say 'let me go' but no sound would come. Tom had a firm grip. He continued to drag and carry her away, back towards the women. He could see her mother, tears streaming down her cheeks, her hands clasped unable to move. Tom picked Amy up and carried her across the green stretch of grass, and placed her gently on the ground beside her mother.

A gunshot rang out. One sharp blast, a slight echo. Then silence. Still lying on the ground, Amy buried her head into her hands curled herself into a small ball and began to whimper. Soft awe full animal sounds slipping out of her, in heart broken, gut-wrenching moans.

Sounds that entered forever into the hearts of the women who gathered around her.

CHAPTER 19

AMY WANDERED ALONG the side of the creek at the back of her home. It was a week since the death of Friska. Everything seemed unnatural, unreal, even walking her legs moved but she felt disconnected from them, just a dull numbness inside. She pulled, unthinking, at the hanging willow branches. She could not bring herself to walk down the path through the ink weed to the hay shed and Friskas paddock.

That evening Katie and Amy had been driven home in a neighbours automobile. She could not remember any of it. She could only hear the gunshot.

At school the other children played their noisy games but would suddenly fall silent when she came near, only to start back into their play as they moved further from her. Pammy never left her side. Neither did Tom. He said nothing. He simply remained near her; his presence providing comfort in a warm, unspoken, understanding way.

Now she just wanted to be away from them all. People who loved her. People whose voices would drop when she came near. Amy lent her back against a tree and gazed into the creek. Clear water ran in an endless, silver streaked movement over the small stones that lay crisp and clear on the bottom. In a hundred years time she thought, this same creek would still be running its never ending course, taking its life giving water to where ever it was going. Amy sighed and moved on through the long grass and finding a log warm in the sun she sat and rested her chin in her hands, watching the water spread out into a small pool where the creek wound its way around a corner.

How stupid it was to believe in God. What an absolute misguided trick of mankind to make up something like God. Darwin was right with his theory of evolution the world was just something that happened. Just exploded out of a some far distant time that spat the earth into space. And then long slow evolution gradually created all things and species. When slowly Apes became humans. How stupid it all was. And how fooled people were. Her mother and father went to church. She had loved going with them but now?? I can never go again she thought. It is all just a made up myth to make people be good. Well it certainly works in that way. Amy sighed a long sigh. How pathetic it all was. How pointless.

There was a rustling in the grass and suddenly a warm body pushed up against her and a damp nose sniffed against her hand. Amy reached out and felt the warm, furry body of Razz, her fathers' favourite dog.

"Hello Razz," she whispered. The dog sidled around in front of her, his brown and gold fur blending with the sunlight on the grass, he dropped his body down low, folding his legs beneath him and wriggled forward placing his chin on her knees and looking up at her. Amy ran her hand over his head and Razz dropped his ears down in a smiling reply. The dog thumped his tail on the ground and as she rubbed his ear his tail thumping increased.

"What is it all about Razz? "she asked him gently. "We are born and we live and we work and we die. It just makes no sense. People always seem to be struggling. Look at some of my friends parents with their rough hands and tired faces. How sad they mostly look. How pathetic it is to hear the Vicar tell everyone who attends church week after week that they need to have their sins forgiven. They have not even committed any sins. All the sinners don't go to the church. God is just a big HAVE made up to make us good."

Razz wriggled closer and Amy ran her hand over his body. How amazing it is she thought, how his fur grows so intricately and correctly from his skin. Millions of small hairs growing from somewhere. He opened his mouth and his long tongue fell panting from between strong white teeth. Did dogs hunt like foxes and wolves once? Why do you pant? Does it cool you down under that fur coat? And your body is full of veins and blood vessels that run with great order and precision feeding your heart and muscles making you strong and fast and you constantly work, on and on and on when you hear my fathers commands and obey them.

Razz slipped from her knees and rolled over his four legs draped toward the sky, she leaned over and rubbed his belly, what does it all mean Razz? Look how beautiful the trees are growing beside the stream, their leaves are golden, some are red, and they are dropping them down for the winter. See how the trees pull nourishment up from below the ground, and it runs up that great trunk in millions of tiny veins feeding the entire tree, not unlike you and me Razz. But how does the tree know when it is summer or winter, when to grow leaves and when to drop them? How does that fit in to all of this beautiful order. Is that what it is? Order? The tide comes in and out, you and I breathe in and out, the tree breaths through its leaves, why is dog, God spelt backwards? Is it because you are faithful and loyal, that you are so full of love for humans?

Suddenly Razz stood up pricking his ears forward with all his attention now directed back down the path. He looked at Amy dropping his ears.

"It is all right Razz, you can go." she told him and the dog, every cell in his body now tuned in another direction, began to trot away. Amy followed him.

Completely disconnected from her, Razz jogged ahead down the path, his head erect and listening. Amy followed as they came out from the trees to where her father was working with his Clydesdale horses out in an open paddock. The two horses were harnessed to a double plough and Doug was guiding them skilfully down the lines of freshly turned earth, ploughing up the paddock for a winter crop. They made a beautiful sight. The great horses were tuned in with understanding of the man. Hundreds of birds, small and large were following them and feasting on the grubs and beetles that the newly turned ground exposed. Razz hopped through the fence and trotted off towards his master.

Amy leaned on the fence. How beautiful the horses were. They were doing the work that they had been bred to do. Did they evolve? What instinct had triggered inside Razz that he knew his master was there. There had been no sounds to let him know. What instinct had told Amy that Friska could beat larger horses in the Ladies Mile Steeplechase? She turned around and looked back at the trees. Their gold and red leaves falling gently one by one, she looked towards the stream, it was hiding now below its banks she could just hear it, she looked back at her father and his beautiful working horses, can this all just happen? Such precision? And what then was love? Razz completely loved her father. The horses completely loved her father. They listened, they tuned in to him, they loved to obey his bidding. Was this God? How could love just happen.

From somewhere inside Amy something went SNAP. She could never explain it. It was just a knowledge, just an immediate glimpse of something very very great. As if some huge stone of ignorance had been suddenly rolled away exposing a missing piece. Why, she thought, Darwin missed the boat. He did not look far enough. All of this could not have just happened. It is too complex, too magnificent. Nowhere does he discuss the soul. The dog has a soul, as does the tree. We have instinct. It is as if some huge intelligence, a master mind beyond anything we understand is at work fine tuning and guiding. Is that intelligence called God? We have to call it something.

Amy leaped into the air. She turned and raced back down the path beside the stream. She turned four cartwheels in a row, dancing with delight. YES she told herself. YES.... we can't just have happened, because there is just too much world of spirit, of soul, of love. The hairs that lie covering the back of Razz are too many and too precise. It is too much to have all just happened, so that means that someone, something, some creative intelligence has made it. Made it so magnificently beautiful it is almost too much too understand. There is a spirit world that works with us, unseen and loving. Huia understands it. She lives in both worlds at once, spirit and real, what knowledge that must give. Spirit is actually great unseen intelligence.

Amy danced with delight. So Friska is not just a piece of meat lying under the cold ground he is dancing in the spirit world. Never had Amy felt such joy. The dark cloud that had settled over her head and shoulders simply rolled away, leaving a lightness that made her feel as if she walked three feet above the ground. After so many days of such unspeakable sadness Amy felt lighter than the air around her.

I don't know what it all means, she whispered to herself. I just know that it is alright...

CHAPTER 20

Tom was surprised to find his father waiting at the school gate. His father never came to the school, yet now, in the mid afternoon and with school over for the day, there was his father leaning on the gate post waiting.

"Dad. What are you doing here? Is something wrong?"

"No son. No. I want to talk with your friend Joseph. Is he here today? Have I missed him? How is Amy, she getting on all right?" Joe could not keep the anxious note from his voice when he asked of Amy.

"She is totally different today Dad. She is ...er ... happy. She is ... well yes, happy. I'll go and find Joseph."

Joe walked back towards the village between the two boys. He asked after Huia and then of Joseph's family as the many children, freed from the school day, headed in all directions towards their homes, laughing and talking, their school bags strapped on their backs. He waited until they had run off and the noise had died away.

"Joseph," he put his hand on the young one's shoulder. "You now own a house."

With a sudden jerk, Joseph stopped in his tracks. He stared at Joe and slowly, as the news took hold, he seemed to grow two inches taller. The knowledge the older man brought him settled deeply into him, then a grin, that started in his very toes, came out on his face, growing bigger by the minute. Joseph threw his school bag high into the air and with a loud whoop, he grabbed the older man by the arms and danced in circles around in the centre of the road.

"Come on," said Joe grinning at his eagerness. "Let's go and have a look, shall we?"

The house sat in a half-acre of ground on the corner of the main road and the street that led to the church. Lank grass, dotted with weeds, decorated their view, and at the rear from a tall flowering gum tree, dangled a child's swing, the seat lying crooked and unused. Peeling paint was flaking off the walls. A piece of gutter had broken, pointing up to the sky like some crazy, upside down boot. Suddenly, and for no reason, all three of them burst out laughing as if together they saw the potential of a sunny, happy home. Joseph ran down the dirt path jumping onto the verandah that spread itself across the front of the house. He gazed in the window as Joe walked up behind him, took a key from his pocket and placed it in Joseph's hand.

Inside, they looked into everything. The house had not been used for some years and appeared forgotten and shabby, but it was warm, dry and sound. A large living room, four bedrooms and a wide kitchen that opened onto a back porch and stepped out onto the large overgrown backyard.

"Look," said the excited Joseph. "A stove. A real, dinkum, wood stove. My mum will be beside herself! AND... can you believe this? A BATHROOM..."

Finally, full inspection over, all three sat down on the back step and looked happily on the weeds and fern that spread over the grass.

"There's something else," said Joe quietly as he pulled a roll of paper from his pocket. "This," he added. "Is a bill of ownership. I had to sign it on your behalf and make myself into a trustee of your affairs. Y'see you're a minor, and as such, cannot own property until you are eighteen so the Deed is written for the ownership to revert to you on your eighteenth birthday."

Joseph's eyes filled. His whole being felt choked with tears of joy.

"Er – that's not all," Joe added. He pulled several pound notes from his pocket and handed them to Joseph. The young Maori looked at him, unsure and surprised.

"What's this?"

"It's yer change. The house cost thirty five pounds. The church no longer wants it so they were happy to sell it below cost. It should cost about ten or twelve quid to get it fixed and painted. That'll leave you plenty for furniture, you know, beds and tables and chairs and stuff. I'll bet your Mum would love a copper. There is an old wash house against the far fence and y'could if you wanted to get a tank stand up and some water laid on, there is only that old fashioned pump in the garden but it brings good water up from the hidden well."

Joseph, money in hand, stood and looked down on the two sitting on the step. His best friend, and a pakeha at that, and his friend's father. How right he had been to trust older Joe. Joseph looked up into the gum tree its flowers almost over as the late autumn closed, the abandoned childrens swing hanging at its crazy angle from a lower branch, the late afternoon sun dancing its weakening rays through the leaves. He felt the strange, heavy burden inside him dissolve. It simply flowed from him leaving his body through his solar plexus, it made him feel light. Joseph straightened; he felt tall; he felt wonderful; he felt like a man.

"You have done me and my family a very great favour," he said quietly. "I do not know how we can ever repay you. I know that for the rest of my life, I will never forget what you have done for us."

Joe shrugged, slightly embarrassed, but aware of the sincere and honest meaning of the young Maori, not wanting to take this moment from him. Not wanting to interfere with his need to express his heart.

"You have repaid me in full Joseph. Just to see how you have grown into the honourable man you are, is repayment enough."

CHAPTER 21

THEY WERE SITTING at the large kitchen table when he came. Sipping tea and enjoying Katie's freshly baked cupcakes. The room was warm with the mid-winter fire and the late afternoon sun barely made it into the room through the west windows.

Razz and the farm dogs gave the alarm as jumping from their favourite spot on the wide verandah, they ran, yapping and growling, out to the road.

"We had better take a look. Don't know what could've set them off." said Doug, trying very hard not to burst into a grin, he struggled to keep his face straight as they all left the kitchen.

Joe Sigley was riding down the road on a grey mare. She stood tall, around fifteen hands high, and carried herself as if the road beneath her feet, was paved in diamonds, designed just for her. Reluctantly, as he was enjoying the ride, Joe reigned her to a stop at their roadside gate and he looked down into three pairs of eyes all fastened expectantly on him. Doug, his friend, whose eyes sparkled knowingly, Katie, whose eyes were apprehensive, and Amy, whose green/blue eyes took in the horse, hungrily devouring every line of the beautiful animal.

"Well... Can a man get a cup of tea around here or not? What kind of neighbours just stand there gawking?" Joe swung off the horse and handed Amy the reins. "Be a champ and tie her up in a good spot for me Amy." He rubbed his backside. "A man's bones get older all the time."

Amy led the tall grey through to the paddock behind the house. Once out of site of the others she stopped and studied the beautiful animal. This, she thought, is the most stately horse I have ever seen.

You're a phantom. A grey, dancing, beautiful phantom she whispered as she ran her hand over the mare, feeling across her shoulders, and down the strong, fine legs. The mare tossed her head and snorted, her tail swished, long and expressive, showing her pleasure. She had a deep, wide chest a sure sign of strength, her hind quarters were sleek and strong. All points led to her black legs from the dapple grey of her coat to her newly shod hooves.

Amy leaned into her neck. She loved the smell of her. For a brief moment she had a sharp pang of pain for her lost pony, then, rubbing the ears of Joe's horse, she tethered her to the fence and turned back to the house.

The two men and Katie sat at the kitchen table where more tea was being sipped.

"Ah," grunted Joe. "Well? What do you think?"

"Oh she is a beautiful mare. How long have you had her? She is such a show horse, will you use her on your farm?"

"I would say there is some Arab in her. Got those fine legs and deep chest a real Arab sign. They say they are bred to run through desert sand and I must say that I saw a few of 'em when I was in Egypt during th' Great War and what wonderful horses they were, small and strong and fast, I never saw horses run like them. Y'have to see those endless hills of desert sand to understand a bit about them."

Amy gazed down at her fingernails. She suddenly felt very strange. A small, familiar urge rose in her, an urge she could not resist. It unfolded within her in a strong, warm longing.

"I wonder, well. er… would you mind if I took her for a small ride." She blushed and felt embarrassed. "I mean, well it would only be once around the paddock just to see how she handles, she looks young, not really experienced, so I would be very careful."

Joe gazed at her. He had to swallow hard before he could speak. He glanced at Doug sitting beside him, his face reflecting both anguish and anticipation.

"Your father and I found her at the Pukekohe sale last week and she travelled in by train this morning." His voice was a whisper.

"And she is for you Amy. We bought her for you.

END

GLOSSARY

Billies	large light water containers, used in early times to boil water
Birdcage	small enclosed area, built to parade horses for show before a race.
Quid	slang for one pound
Guinea	one pound and ten shillings/ twenty one shillings.
Hongi	Maori tradition of pressing noses transfer of life force between two people.
Hu ha	nonsense
Karakia	Maori prayer or chant
Koru	an elegant design of a curve.
Kuia	grandmother /old woman
Mana	prestige/honour
Marae	Maori meeting house
Maori	a native of New Zealand.
Moko	a tattoo
Mokupuna	grandchild
Ngapuhi	northern Maori tribes of New Zealand
Pa	Maori village
Pakeha	pale skinned/white man/foreigner
Rangitira	noble one/Chieftan line
Reinga	northern end of New Zealand, sacred to Maori as the place of departing spirits.

Slump	slang for the great depression of the early 1930's.
Steeplechase	a race over hurdles or fences.
Taniwha	a serpent or God like spirit
Tapu	sacred
Tohunga	priest
Tua tua	small shellfish
Tui	melodious native bird
Tupuna	ancestors
Utu	revenge

In 1935 Amy was fourteen years old. Her storey is of her home life and friendships, her school, how her friends lived and most of all, how she thought as a teenager in a different way of life from today. Society and its external additions may change, but the human heart remains as it always has.